THE CREAM PACKARD

THE CREAM PACKARD

James Avis

Copyright © 2018 James Avis

The moral right of the author has been asserted.

Apart from any fair dealing for the purposes of research or private study, or criticism or review, as permitted under the Copyright, Designs and Patents Act 1988, this publication may only be reproduced, stored or transmitted, in any form or by any means, with the prior permission in writing of the publishers, or in the case of reprographic reproduction in accordance with the terms of licences issued by the Copyright Licensing Agency. Enquiries concerning reproduction outside those terms should be sent to the publishers.

This is a work of fiction. Names, characters, businesses, places, events and incidents are either the products of the author's imagination or used in a fictitious manner. Any resemblance to actual persons, living or dead, or actual events is purely coincidental.

Matador
9 Priory Business Park,
Wistow Road, Kibworth Beauchamp,
Leicestershire. LE8 0RX
Tel: 0116 279 2299
Email: books@troubador.co.uk
Web: www.troubador.co.uk/matador
Twitter: @matadorbooks

ISBN 978 1788038 003

British Library Cataloguing in Publication Data.
A catalogue record for this book is available from the British Library.

Printed and bound by CPI Group (UK) Ltd, Croydon, CR0 4YY
Typeset in 13pt Adobe Garamond Pro by Troubador Publishing Ltd, Leicester, UK

Matador is an imprint of Troubador Publishing Ltd

For Rose Anne, with cherished memories

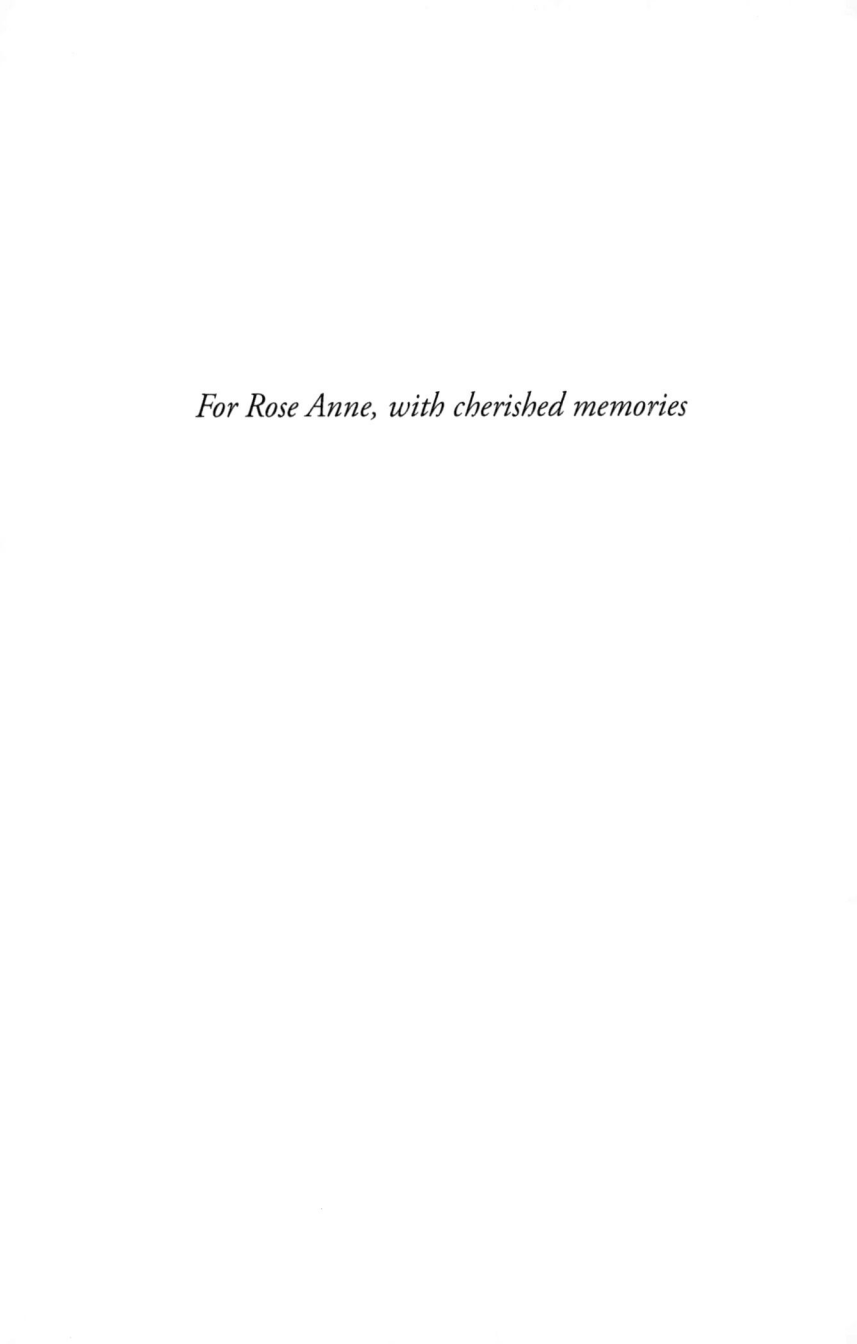

Acknowledgements

My gratitude to dear Marie F. Wasie and her grandnephew Gregg D. Sjoquist for their generous hospitality during my first visit to America and unforgettable Minnesota.

A special thank you to Mary Helen Lorenz who introduced me to all things American.

My gratitude to Donnie Crevier and Larry Anderson of Crevier Classic Cars Mesa, California for their kind and generous assistance.

My gratitude to Dean Kirkland of Dean Kirkland Photography and Film Production, Santa Ana, California for the exceptional photos of this very special Packard Automobile.

* * *

A sincere thank you to those friends who have made a significant contribution to the writing of this novel:

Michael Slack, Else Bublies, Gobi Gopalakrishnan, Cherie Silver, Thomas O. Marshall, Maxine Taylor, Keith Moodie, Billy Ansar, John Bath, Bruce Blevins.

Contents

1. Sentimental Journey – Elaine Mason 1
2. The Wedding 3
3. The Interview – Matt Johnson 10
4. The Drugstore – Barbara Hogarth 14
5. Shrink – Caroline Mason 18
6. Hotel Rendezvous 22
7. Photo Shoot 28
8. Country Club – Vera Pilcher 33
9. Blue Eyes – Britt Lisell 36
10. The Mimosa – Frankie Bernstein 40
11. Blue Sails 46
12. Auction – Nick Carter 51
13. Care Home – Mary Christie 56
14. Baseball 61
15. Care Home – From Here to Eternity 68
16. The Blue House 75
17. The Cream Packard 79
18. Pink Sapphires – Murky and Bimbo 84
19. Pink Sapphires – The Deal 89
20. State Fair 95
21. Double Cross 98

22.	Dead or Alive – Doc Quaid	102
23.	Autopsy – Clarence Larson	106
24.	Julie	108
25.	The Alibi	111
26.	Man Bites Dog	115
27.	Sunfish	118
28.	FBI – Novak and Petersen	120
29.	Funeral	123
30.	Body Snatchers – Nick Carter	125
31.	Happy Days – Warren Clarke	128
32.	First Love – Nick Carter	131
33.	The Setup	134
34.	The Fix	136
35.	Sweet Revenge – Carla Santiago	142
36.	Front Page	145
37.	Au Revoir	147
38.	Farewell Minnesota	150
39.	Message – Nick Carter	152
40.	Memories	154

SENTIMENTAL JOURNEY
– ELAINE MASON

An ocean of yellow flowers embraced an undulating Minnesota. It was a long way down, but I could just make out the deep ochre colours of those traditional Dutch barns that used to be so familiar. I was heading home… Earlier that morning, before sunrise, I piloted my single engine Cessna 180 from a small airfield near San Bernardino. So far, the flight had been easy, almost monotonous, but that sudden visual impact reminded me that yellow was still my favourite colour. The controls were adjusted as I flew lower to reassure myself I had made the right decision. Travelling east the brilliant sunshine began to pick out familiar lakes, some small, graduating to larger ones, with anglers fishing from clinker-built boats.

THE CREAM PACKARD

It was late August 1956. Ten years earlier, ambition had taken me to Hollywood. The war in the Pacific had just ended and I wanted a slice of new action. Besides… dad suddenly died and things were not the same. Mother remarried and her new spouse and daughter moved in. At first we all got on, but before long I needed my own space, and a career to match my extravagant tastes.

To begin with, it was a struggle against fierce competition, but with determination, lots of luck, and a little more besides, I slowly clawed my way up the slimy Hollywood ladder to get an Oscar nomination for my last film. I learned success was always bitter sweet.

Without warning, I overshot Lake Minnetonka, so took a steep arc left, just cleared a group of conifer, skirted the perimeter of the lake, and pointed the chassis back towards the mooring. The first attempt was a failure, but gave a welcome glimpse of the 'Big White House', partially hidden by Sugar Maple, alongside the obligatory 'stars and stripes' attached to a painted flagpole.

THE WEDDING

Johnson got an invite to the wedding. At least, let's say he got hold of an invitation, and turned up at the lakeside home of the bride's parents, known locally as the Big White House. No one knew how he got there, but, out of mild politeness, nobody cared.

The ceremony had taken place earlier that Saturday, in a small Catholic Church, and after the usual round of photographs, which seemed to go on forever, the guests returned for the reception around a swimming pool in the magnificent grounds and manicured lawns that stretched down to the lake. He deliberately avoided the tedious photocall, and made a mental note for *his* photos to be taken *prior* to any ceremony, should he ever get married.

Looking across to the lake, he saw the outline of

a large boat, moored in a private jetty. Someone had taken the time and expense to erect a frame to protect it… way beyond his meagre salary as a hack reporter for the *Minneapolis Star*.

Cars arrived, as Johnson walked along the drive towards the house. Occupants spilled onto the lawns, eager to take advantage of all on offer. One guest, dripping in vulgar jewellery, emerged from her chauffeur driven silver Cadillac Eldorado Biarritz convertible, with wrap-around windshield, all smothered in chrome. He got a glimpse of the impressive two-tone green and white leather interior. Several others, mostly males, eager for attention, crowded around her. Even at a distance, Johnson could detect this "dame" knew how to milk an audience. Her name was Vera Pilcher.

Circling the pool were tables covered in ivory linen and silver service, groaning from an overload of food. One table was devoted to exotic fruit. A white trellis, covered in silk bows and gardenia, provided a classy backdrop and enclosure. One or two adventurous types, with lean curvaceous figures, had already ventured into the water. Reflections of afternoon sunlight danced against the blue mosaic pattern decorating the pool's edge.

Johnson moved closer to the food. Considering the awkward hours he worked, being single was an advantage, but he missed good cooking. He made the most of the occasion and copied the mid-west custom by stuffing anything and everything onto one plate, including a portion of chocolate gateaux covered in fresh cream. He added a fork with napkin and slowly examined the guests. The actress had to be there... he needed this story.

With his free hand he captured a strawberry daiquiri cocktail from a passing tray, and mingled. The guests looked and smelled rich. They were from all parts of the State and beyond. He heard several Texan drawls and other voices from Carolina. The afternoon sunshine got too hot so he shed his jacket and tie, then moved into the cool shade of nearby overhanging willows.

'Would you like some?'

Johnson turned to face a slim, suntanned and energetic girl in a peach 'Catalina' one piece bathing costume. His eyes followed all the curves. She stood there with an outstretched arm attached to a large plate. Her piercing green eyes matched a wide mischievous grin. He added more cake to his collection.

'Have you finished your swim?'

'For now,' she replied.

'Shouldn't you get dressed?'

'Why...do you think I'm provocative?' Before he could reply, she added, 'Let me introduce myself. I'm Caroline Mason. That's my stepsister over there. The one with the veil.' A hint of sarcasm crept in.

'Are you jealous?'

'Hell no! Colby's a doctor, not my type, but useful. I know where to go when I get a snake bite!'

'Gee... you have snakes as well, on top of all this?'

'A few, usually about your size... they turn up at weddings uninvited and scoff all the food!'

He took the hit. 'What happened to your guest, Elaine Mason?'

'Why do you ask?'

'A small town boy like me wants to meet a celluloid queen close up.'

She gave him a disappointed look. 'And here I am, thinking all along you wanted a second helping of my cake!' She pushed the plate into the nearest waiter, grabbed her bathrobe, threw it over one shoulder, and moved away towards the house. 'Keep your eyes on the lake,' she called back.

**

'Can you manage all that?'

Johnson turned to face a fit-looking young man, with an engaging smile and unfamiliar accent.

'Are you from these parts?'

'Good Lord no, flew in from London a couple of days ago... invited to the Wedding. Super show, don't you think? Oh, forgive me, I'm Nick Carter. Are you a real reporter? Never met one before, and in case you are wondering, Caroline told me.'

'You mean she knew all along?'

'Well, I wasn't sure, but you aren't dressed for the occasion, and ask a lot of questions.'

Johnson frowned, but knew he had to confide in someone to get sufficient information for a scoop, albeit a local one.

'Tell me about her...tell me about Elaine Mason.'

'She's been away some time. I'm as keen as you are to meet a famous actress. Caroline says she has the most beautiful cream *Packard*. She loves that car and won't let anyone drive it. It is garaged where she left it, but I haven't seen it... don't even know what a *Packard* looks like. Guess it must be big, like everything else around here!'

In that moment, there was the faint sound of a light aircraft approaching overhead. Johnson shaded his eyes against the sun, and looked into the clear blue Minnesota sky. As it passed over a second time the wedding party emerged from the marquee and moved towards the lake. On a second approach the undercarriage floats hit the surface of the water and scattered a flock of mallard duck. The landing left a trail of foam and bubbles which sparkled in the bright sunshine. The aircraft taxied across the water to the wooden jetty. The engine switched off, and peace returned to the lake. Elaine Mason emerged from the cockpit to a ripple of applause. Caroline returned dressed, still drying her hair.

'Just like her…she loves a dramatic entrance. Nick, go down and secure the plane to the jetty. Make sure she doesn't damage the boat.'

Nick eagerly obliged, quickly placed his drink on a nearby table, and made sure he was the first to meet and greet his famous cousin.

'Bring her across to the marquee,' she called after him. Nick escorted the actress through the waiting guests. She signed a couple of autographs, ignored the rest, and presented the bride with a wedding gift secured with white satin ribbon. Warren Clarke, accustomed to public speaking, gave a Champagne toast to the happy couple who cut the cake. Johnson returned to his grilled lobster.

'Freshen your drink, sir?' A waiter in a red waistcoat offered more cocktail from a cut glass container, adding a sprig of fresh mint. 'Sure glad she made it safely,' he added. 'Last time she crash-landed we were eating mallard clear through to Christmas!'

The Interview
– Matt Johnson

I never met Elaine Mason on Saturday, but cleverly arranged a meeting for Sunday afternoon. Nick Carter brokered the deal and I grabbed a slice of good fortune. From the outside, it looked like a combination of naivety and English good manners, or that the 'Queen' had taken a liking to one of her subjects. In reality, I promised Nick an exclusive photo of his celebrity cousin. He liked that. The problem was that I didn't have any, but phoned Debbie at the *Star*. She worked nights, so I persuaded her to extract a selection for Mac the Editor, from our Press Archives, and one for Nick. Debbie never came cheap. I promised her a ticket to the next Presley concert. She would have a long wait. Elvis had just performed at the Auditorium, three months earlier, and never returned.

Most of Sunday morning was spent in bed, allowing Saturday's consumption of alcohol to vaporate. Suddenly the phone rang. It was Mac, who habitually terminated all things nice. He could always spot a weakness.

'You awake? Then listen up. Those shots you sent were lousy. Were you using a camera? I'm sending Hogarth!'

Lost for words and in a state of seizure and hurt pride, my reply went something like this… 'Mac, how can you do this to me? She's a rookie. Don't you realise the importance of this spread?'

The reply came swift and decisive. 'Best we can offer…rest of us are covering a homecoming for our boys, from Korea. Make do with Hogarth; she can handle a camera, besides, she's already on her way!'

* * *

Late Sunday afternoon I picked her up in my Ford woody station wagon as she got off the bus from Minneapolis. In hot, dry and dusty weather, without air conditioning, her journey had been long and tedious. They hadn't given her a car, she was not that important. On the drive over to the boarding house, I divulged a few details.

'Mac asked me to do this 'special'. It's small bananas compared to Hollywood gossip, but big news for this county.' In truth, I needed this one badly, especially after my last fiasco. Mac assigned me to cover the opening of a new Maternity Ward by the Mayor's wife. By coincidence she was expecting their firstborn at that time. I screwed up! Somehow the photo on the front page of the *Star* showed the Mayor's mistress, instead of his wife. The inappropriate caption read… *'First Lady delivery due soon!'*

After Hogarth had unpacked, freshened up, and powdered her nose more times than Babe Ruth hit home runs, we left for the Big White House, and arrived shortly after seven. We were shown inside by Marcia Clarke, Elaine's mother. The sound of Morgan Lewis's 'How High the Moon' came from a piano in a far corner of the room. On approach, Elaine Mason stopped playing and crossed over to meet us. I should have worn Indian 'snow shoes' to negotiate the deep pile carpet. She offered cigarettes and lit one for herself with a gold lighter which she returned to her purse. As I fumbled, and eventually connected, blue smoke drifted slowly upwards into the wide expanse of this enormous room.

Mason disarmed us with a charming, inquisitive smile, and offered tea, which we politely declined. My questions were trimmed to suit our mid-west readers… nothing too technical. She made it clear from the outset that her personal life was strictly private, and in her words "off limits". Contentious issues were cleverly sidelined, but she was forthcoming for the most part, which I thought was refreshing.She enthused about her latest success and sought our opinion.

The interview took little over an hour. Hogarth took photos against a backdrop of carefully arranged pink and white gladioli. It was all cordial, if unspectacular. There were so many flowers in the room, Hogarth thought the bill eclipsed her monthly salary.

THE DRUGSTORE
– BARBARA HOGARTH

As an only child from a hard working family out of Cincinnati, Barbara Hogarth had already shouldered her share of responsibility by working on the family farm. After hard knocks gained with a minor Chicago newspaper, and a brief romance, which fell apart, she moved west for a fresh challenge. An overnight stop and shortage of funds prompted a temporary stay in Minneapolis, where she got a job. Hogarth was stubborn but determined. For now, her intended trip to Denver would have to wait.

* * *

After leaving Mason, Matt Johnson took me to a nearby Drug Store where we sat down to coffee. Before I joined the *Star*, I had wondered how, with my limited skills, I would keep up with the pace of a major newspaper. After less than a week, I began to think *they* were no match for me. Johnson sounded and looked sluggish for a reporter who had been with this outfit almost ten years.

'Do we have to dine out amongst pills and antiseptic?' I enquired. He looked disappointed.

'It's a Drug Store, what do you expect? And there's a bonus… a 'Pat Boone' track on the Juke Box over there.'

'So why have an eating place in the middle of it?' He looked and sounded annoyed.

'You've been too long in Chicago. This little offshoot is part of American folklore.' He went on to explain. 'A small town like Excelsior can't sustain two separate stores, it's not viable, so they double up as one. It makes sense.'

Matt was doing his best sales pitch, but I remained unimpressed. 'Pick a different venue next time, or you might find a corn plaster in your doughnut!'

'Listen and learn Miss Hogarth,' he retorted. 'Some local customs go back to pioneering days and the first settlers. As wagon trains moved west, they travelled with only essentials, mostly food and water. Log cabins and fences were built without nails. One particular style of fencing was called "split rail". There are many variations. They joined corners with dowels that were driven into wood. Some straight, with stacked corners and posting, but many were built in a zigzag fashion, to add strength.'

'Excelsior was settled around 1850, only ten years before the Civil War. Compared to most European cities that's almost brand new. The vast plains, impossible terrain, and harsh climate made access difficult, until the first locomotive arrived. Somehow people survived, they had to. The earliest settlers were Indian. In case you were wondering, "Minnetonka" is Dakota Indian, and means "Great Water".'

I felt chastened, had misjudged my companion and quickly tried to make amends. 'Thanks for the lecture, Professor. I'm impressed. Have you studied these customs?'

'Not in any depth, but a good reporter should have an inbuilt curiosity, about most things. Did you get some good shots tonight?' he asked, keen to subdue any further dispute.

I was no pushover, so looked him square on and gave no ground. 'The photos will make Mac purr, a little, but it was all too dry, wasn't it? Like Death Valley on a Sunday. Look Matt, that was a cover up. The real story is still out there. You struck out, zonked by her long suntanned legs and traffic-light-red painted toenails. We know nothing about Elaine Mason, or anything that might appeal to our readers. This is nowhere near ready for copy. Go tell Mac we need more time… blame the delay on the actress.'

Before he could respond, Shelli the waitress appeared. 'Anything else for you folks?'

'The bill', I replied, 'and he's the one on expenses!'

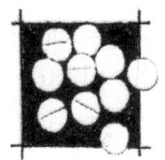

Shrink
– Caroline Mason

'I suppose it all started after Dad died in that car crash. I was young at the time and the shock cut deep. It still hurts. I leant on Elaine for a while, then after she left for Hollywood my days were all too empty. Yes…I was jealous of her success, which created one long bitter void. Nothing seemed to fit anymore.'

'There were a few high school dates, which always ended in the cold back seat of a car, usually at a drive-in Movie. I guess I wasn't ready for that kind of stuff. I became confused and no 'paper shaker'.'

'After school, I drifted, even worked at the drug store. None of it meant much, and I sure didn't need the money. Dad left me a generous allowance. I'm Sagittarius…we can't handle money. Spendthrift, that's me. Mom is always telling me off for buying things in two's and threes. Even bought a gypsy red Chevy Corvette only last year. Loved that fast car… but she sent it back for a refund. I can't help it. If there is money around, I have to spend it, no matter what! Once I bought a boy a motor cycle for his birthday. It was a Harley Davidson. Guess I wanted to impress him. A week later his dad brought it back and said his son ought not to have accepted it. Joe was drafted shortly after and got killed, driving a supply truck in Korea. Doesn't make sense, does it?'

'Mom and I used to get along, but since my illness things have been volcanic. She got fed up and went down to Mexico for a long vacation. Her friends said she was cracking up. Can you imagine that? And I'm the one on medication! While she was away, they dumped me in a clinic for six weeks. Even gave me 'shock' treatment. Don't recall much, but my jaw ached for a while. The others seemed a lot worse than me. One guy took a light bulb into the treatment room and stuck it in his ear. Reckons he got a flicker. Can you believe that?'

'No…I don't trust anyone, not since Dean departed. We had a good thing going, regular dates and all. He even took me to meet his folks in Wisconsin… then it all fell apart. I brought him home to meet Mom, and over lunch he blurts out that he's already engaged to a girl he met at high school. Can you imagine that? I was too shocked to be embarrassed, nobody believed my end of it, for God's sake!'

'There is another guy I like, and he likes me. I know this because he buys me gifts and things. We don't go out much… he's older than me. No… I don't want to say anymore.'

'The illness is worse nights, that's why I read a lot, mostly romantic novels or "notions" as I call them. Silly isn't it?… Little miss action, tuned into "sugar and spice". Sometimes I can't cope with it all and feel like ending this hell. There is no relief. If you have never suffered, you can't contemplate the torment. You can't see it or taste it, can hardly describe it, and worst of all, I can't get rid of it. It's like living in a shoebox, and now and again some kind soul lifts the lid a fraction to share a splash of sunshine.'

'One or two close to me know I suffer, but it's painful for them too. Sometimes my outrageous remarks dig deep into emotions. I'm surprised people tolerate my behaviour. Maybe it all reflects the Sagittarius in me. I'm generous, but God knows where all the rest of this shit comes from. Manic depression is cruel, isn't it? Those tablets you gave me are pure torment. They keep me awake all night, so I'm sleeping all day. Who feeds the horses and walks my dog?'

The Psychiatrist stopped taking notes, removed her glasses, placed the writing pad and fountain pen on the desk, and switched off the recorder.

'That will be all for now Caroline. Take this scrip to the Pharmacy. I've changed your medication. Your next appointment is the same time next Monday, a week today.'

Hotel Rendezvous

The weekend was over and the reality of a dismal Monday night set in. Against dark, overhanging clouds it began to rain… dense heavy rain, the sort the midwest offers after a long dry period of drought. At a distance, across the lake, shafts of jagged lightening hit the ground, silhouetting the boarding house.

The road outside was isolated until a dark maroon Ford Woody station wagon pulled up alongside and a figure entered. He shed water from his wide brimmed hat, rushed upstairs, and knocked on a bedroom door. Hogarth emerged in a bathrobe from a shower at the end of the corridor.

'Quick, bring your camera, I'll be waiting in the wagon.'

'Your timings lousy,' she was about to say, but

his urgency convinced her to dress quickly and rush downstairs. She jumped into the front seat, as he drove off at speed.

'I was driving past the gas station and spotted a cream coloured car at the pumps. There is only one Packard in these parts and I am sure Elaine Mason is driving it. Something must have spooked her to be driving alone on a night like this. Have you brought your camera?'

A wave of rainwater across the windscreen made it difficult for the wipers to compete. Out in front, the dim red lights of the Packard were barely visible, and at times disappeared altogether, as the vehicle twisted through dense woodland along the edge of the lake.

'Can't you go any faster?' broke in Hogarth. 'We are losing her!' 'Not in these conditions… but relax, this road has only one destination; it leads to the only hotel on the lake.' They arrived and parked discreetly, a short distance from the main entrance. Johnson cut the ignition. Hogarth adjusted her beret, drew up the collar of her raincoat, and stepped into the downpour.

'Wait here. It's my turn, leave this to me.'

By now he was getting used to orders ; he didn't like it, but was content to lean back into the deep leather driving seat and switch on the radio. He made a mental note to have Hogarth on his side should his Landlord try and screw him for unpaid rent. The motor was a second hand 1947 Super deluxe 8 Ford Woody Station Wagon. It had cost more than six months salary to restore the original Tucson paintwork, white wall tyres, chrome work, varnished maple wood and ribbon mahogany panels.

It was an old hotel, almost invisible, save for a red neon sign out front. Rainwater on faulty wiring created a hissing steam. Inside, the rooms had high ceilings and peeling paintwork. The dining area tables were covered in stained red check table cloths and doubled as a bar in the evenings. Only an elderly couple, who had finished what looked like a poor excuse for a meal, occupied the space. She sat and waited. Through an open hatch came faint sounds of Dean Martin's 'Memories are Made of This'…and they were! The couple got up to leave.

'The barman is through the back,' the old man said. 'We'll let him know you are here.'

It was a good ten minutes before he arrived.

'Sorry to keep you waiting ma'am. Had to get some logs in for the fire, awful night.'

He was aged around fifty with flattened black hair that looked dyed. She knew his excuse was pure fiction. As he came through the revolving door she got a glimpse of a curvaceous waitress smoothing a tight skirt and straightening the seams of her black nylon stockings. *All men were stupid,* she thought. *They had all the advantages before marriage, but few thereafter.* A two year investment any girl makes into snaring a good catch always pays handsome dividends, once she has that precious gold band around her left finger!

'Sorry, the restaurant is closed,' he announced. 'Can I get you a drink?' Before Hogarth could reply, he poured out a Trader Vic's spiced rum and joined her. 'Have this one on the house, you need it after fighting your way through that mess outside. It will ease your latest problem.'

'Oh… you noticed, how clever!'

'Yes, it goes with the territory ; a good barman can always spot trouble. Have a sip and tell me all about it.'

Hogarth leant forward and lowered her voice. 'Can you keep a 'secret'? I mean a *real* secret.'

'Sure,' he replied.

'This is difficult for me, you understand, but it's love, deep passionate Love. The kind that consumes every thought, even when I am asleep. Especially when I am dreaming.'

'Gee…that sounds 'heavy'… can't say I've experienced that kind of lust before!'

'Lust! good God man, I'm not talking about lust, I'm talking about passion!' He was surprised by her outburst and tried to hide it, after all he was a barman… service yes, emotion no.

Hogarth continued. 'Two people came here tonight for a clandestine meeting,' she whispered.

'Don't think so,' he replied. 'The Rotary meet Tuesdays and the Klan don't frequent these parts.'

'No not Rotary, a secret meeting of body and mind. I'm desperately in love with one of them. We have been together four years.'

'Sorry ma'am, can't help you there, besides, I did not recognise the Lady, if you are after her name.'

'This may come as a surprise barman, but I want the name of the person who met her here tonight.' He looked disappointed, like when a gorilla is offered a lemon instead of a banana.

'Oh I get it, you are one of those naughty ladies who live together and never marry!'

'Afraid so, and I have a very jealous nature.'

'I knew it! You look different…it's the way you wear your hat!'

'Not a hat, more of a beret, but will you help me? I will be eternally grateful.'

This confession clinched it for Hogarth, but she made a mental note to discard the beret at the first opportunity. 'His name is Warren Clarke, recognised him from his election posters ; ran for Senator a while back. Now clear off ; I want to keep the license.'

She quickly left, crossed the wet drive to the wagon and got inside. Johnson had fallen asleep, but woke at the sound of the door closing.

'You have been a long time, did you learn anything?'

'Some things take a little longer than others,' came the reply.

Photo Shoot

Tuesday provided a better day. The overnight rain had gone, and warm early morning sunshine quickly dried out the sidewalks. It was going to be hot again, and Barbara Hogarth wished she had brought a change of cottons. She phoned Elaine Mason on the pretext that her first photos were not a success and was invited to the boat on the lake. It was a poor excuse. She gambled that Mason, hungry for success, could not resist any sort of publicity, legitimate or otherwise. It all came with territory.

She left Johnson a note and took his vehicle. Without transport he wouldn't be a nuisance. Twenty minutes later she drew a camera from her case and walked to the waters edge. It was an old boat, constructed in teak with a tall mast, and offset with polished brass cleats.

She wondered who did all the cleaning. Nick Carter appeared on deck and engaged with her curiosity.

'The Masons rescued her from Ireland. It's a mystery how they brought her over. Sleeps six and is ocean going, but *The Shannon* won't leave these waters.'

At around six feet, with a lean trim build, Nick was taller than Hogarth. His dark hair contrasted with a pale complexion in need of Minnesota summer sunshine. He was born on the south side of Bromley and spoke with a south London accent acquired when his father started work in a new engineering firm, and moved the family to Croydon. Nick 'bluffed' his way into local Grammar School, but, with two sisters to feed, his education soon became a financial burden, and he left school shortly after his fifteenth birthday. He moved jobs often and talked his way into a salary with a Merchant Bank. At first it amounted to errands and tea making, but he got a break when his boss enlisted him for night school. His father served in the North Africa campaign but was killed in action at Tobruk. It was all too much for his mother who died after the war ended.

Nick thrust out an arm and helped Hogarth on board.

'We met Elaine Sunday, but I'm here for more shots. Are you here on Vacation?' she enquired.

'I suppose I am. Mother died and when I contacted aunt Marcia she invited me to the wedding. As family history goes, Marcia was a nurse and cared for uncle Bradley when he took ill on a business trip to London. They married and settled in Minnesota where his family produced timber. He did well and bought this land.'

'He must have been clever to create all this.'

'Marcia told me he got a survey of the property, which identified a plot with the least mosquitoes, and that is where he built the house. Did you know they breed in the same location every year?'

'So that is why the house is built a distance from the lake.'

'He was unique, but sadly no longer with us. Brad was killed in a car crash a while ago, and aunt Marcia remarried.'

* * *

Elaine Maison appeared on deck. She was dressed informally to suit the occasion and wore a French navy coloured sweater with matching slacks. She gave a five star performance, as Hogarth took more photos. The boat and lake provided a perfect backdrop. As Nick looked on, he thought the flicks at Croydon's Ritz would never again have the same appeal, should he return to London. Following a lengthy photo shoot they sat down on yellow-striped cushioned seats either side of a circular table. Carter would have done anything for a lingering look at his screen goddess, so hung around a while longer serving drinks.

'Ever tasted evil Barbara?'

Hogarth was taken by surprise and quickly discarded her carefully prepared list of notes and questions. She already knew from press gossip that her subject was no angel, and parted company with her studio, after a sordid affair with a well known Film Director. His wife took vengeance. Mason ended up in a swimming pool at a glamorous dinner party… problem was, she was still wearing her mink stole! A second studio propaganda machine mopped up the mess. Reading on…maybe her visit was an escape, and the wedding an excuse. That was always the trouble with rumour, it created more questions than answers.

'I'm in danger,' she whispered.

'Have you contacted the Police?'

'Not yet, with my next movie coming up, scandal is the last thing I need right now.'

'So why talk to me? I'm part of a daily gossip machine called a newspaper.'

'It goes like his. My aircraft engine was sabotaged before takeoff on Saturday. Not enough to stop me flying, but as a cynical reminder. For now, this is between friends, you understand ; should anything happen to me, print the story I am about to tell.'

She offered Hogarth a cigarette. Her hands were trembling as she held her favourite gold Cartier lighter. Suddenly a loud horn sounded from the lake, which made Hogarth jump. An eighteen foot Dart Runabout swept around in an arc, slicing through the shallows, and came alongside. It was a sleek craft with piped seating. Mason's mood changed. She extinguished the cigarette and removed her sunglasses.

'That's Nick... he's taking me to brunch for Joanne and Colby, where they are opening the last of their wedding presents. Let's continue this at the Country Club tonight. Come over at eight, and bring your friend.'

The boat left at speed, leaving a long trail of surface bubbles. Hogarth would have liked to have heard more.

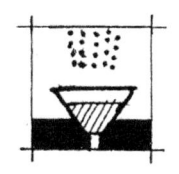

Country Club
– Vera Pilcher

It was half an hour by boat. Warren Clarke offered the wheel to Johnson.

'Is he capable?' Hogarth enquired.

'As long as he keeps to the middle of the lake, well away from the banks and reeds.'

Johnson took the advice and the *The Shannon* moved leisurely ahead at an even pace, manoeuvring along several connecting backwaters and past a pub where customers sat outside at tables, eating, drinking and laughing. It was a warm, breathless evening.

On approach, Clarke retook control and brought the boat alongside a wide, weathered wooden jetty where a suntanned boy wearing a baseball cap grabbed the line and secured it. He helped Barbara and

Caroline disembark and followed on, after giving the boy a modest tip. Marcia Clarke was already inside ; Tuesday was her bridge night. Barbara Hogarth was disappointed, the actress had not turned up.

* * *

Vera Pilcher had a face like a pineapple. A craggy old widow, she had met her husband in Gothenburg from where they eloped as teenagers. After hard beginnings, and more than a few cold winters, they managed to create a wholesale ice cream business with a string of outlets. The venture was sold at a huge profit. Repeating their success made them wealthy.

Since her husband's death Vera has been on a world cruise, and knew every harlot and starlet west of Chicago. She always dressed to kill, or more befitting killed to dress! Her latest acquisitions from Dayton's were an exclusive 'black back' musquash coat and a handbag which had so much snakeskin it almost crawled under the nearest table.

Despite the vulgarity, she was no fool, possessed an electric brain, and was an adept manipulator. She played them all like a slow hand of poker. Johnson recognised her from Saturday's wedding and asked Caroline for an introduction.

'Vera owns that adorable house on the north side, the one in pastel shades with a triple garage.'

'When I am here to enjoy it,' Vera chipped in. 'Most of my time is spent in Miami. Nothing but lawyers since my husband passed on. Had to cope on my own, who can you trust with a dime these days?'

Johnson offered Warren Clarke. Vera abruptly took his arm, drew him aside, and asked Caroline to freshen their drinks from the bar.

'Are you for real? The guys a shyster, tried to sell me a piece of real estate I already owned. Do I look dumb?'

'Was the land in Florida?' Hogarth enquired

'Why yes, how did you know?'

'Wild guess!'

'The man's a criminal. Only went to the wedding because I knew his first wife. He packed Mary off to a Care Home, said she had lost her "marbles and mobility". Never believed a word! She could play a sharp hand of bridge, and you need all your wits for that. Rumour has it she passed away, but only last week I got a letter from her, but no Address.'

BLUE EYES
– BRITT LISELL

Warren Clarke was no fool either. The eldest of five children to Irish immigrants who settled in Harrisburg, his six foot two athletic frame gained him a scholarship to Ivy League Football at Notre Dame. A cartilage injury closed a promising sports career, after which he studied law. Following graduation, and early beginnings at Springfield, Illinois, he moved to Minneapolis St.Paul where he set up his own practice and specialised in real estate to embrace the ongoing expansion of urban sprawl. His first attempt to become a Senator ended in failure.

Clarke remained ambitious, ignored the others, and sat down at one of the tables at the Country Club, to initiate another deal. A waiter approached and handed him a message from a silver salver which read… 'Permission to come on board Captain!' He disguised the urgency, made excuses, quickly rose from the table, and left by a side entrance. On reaching the boat he negotiated the steps down into the cabin.

The faint sounds of Doris Day's 'Love Me or Leave Me' came from a nearby radio. Sitting at a table, he recognised the blonde hair, cold eyes, thin body and long legs under faded jeans. A Patek Philippe watch decorated a left wrist, complemented by a pale blue high neck cashmere sweater. She looked too young to be a Psychiatrist and Director of a local care home. Her name was Britt Lisell.

'I see you got yourself a drink.'

'A girl has to look after herself,' she replied coldly.

'I'll join you.'

He poured himself a Bourbon and offered her another. She declined.

'How long has it been?' he asked.

'Too long… and in case you missed that pitch, too bloody long! Turn back the last page. You got yourself married again, a quick hitch to a rich widow, and, in case you have a memory loss, let me remind you that I'm the one holding the 'baby,' or, to put it another way, nursing your wife.'

'We had an arrangement,' he replied.

'So I see. You move into the mansion while I take the 'heat'. The staff are getting suspicious. A new doctor is asking too many questions. Somehow he got hold of her medical record and has already changed her medication. She'll have to go.'

'You mean transfer?'

'I mean dead, as in corpse.'

'We would never get away with it. Even if…and what about that local Coroner? I hear he is no pushover.'

Lisell gave him a hard, calculating look. 'I never wanted any part of this.'

'You sure didn't operate 'sale or return'. You took the cash, holidays, and a lot more besides.'

Lisell pushed her glass aside and placed both hands on his across the table. Her mood changed. 'What happened to us, Warren? We had it all, those long weekends in Canada… remember that beautiful lakeside cabin.'

'Too late, I'm afraid. The wheel turned when Mary inherited her father's Real Estate. Somehow she found out about us and demanded a divorce. I couldn't let it all slip away.'

'You cheated on her not once, but *three* times. First

with me, then had her certified, and at the end took away her inheritance. How much did you pay that doctor?'

He never answered, but moved across to the drinks cabinet for one more to dull the pain.

'How right you are, always were, did it all for you.'

'Don't you dare say that. This was always about your ego, your greed, your ambition.'

In that moment, Lisell softened. 'It's a mess of your making, but not too late. Return the inheritance to her. You're an attorney, fix it. Get her released, I can help you.'

Clarke got up and opened the cabin door. 'Were it that simple. The land has gone, used to fund crippling debts, including that political mess. Maybe disposing of her is the only way out.'

'You mean murder, why not say it!'

'Yes, I mean murder. Lets talk some more tomorrow, did you bring your toothbrush?'

He returned to the upper deck, released the mooring, and took the boat along the tributary towards the lake. The others would have to find their own way home.

The Mimosa
– Frankie Bernstein

Tuesday was unusually busy for a late night at The Mimosa restaurant, Lakeside. Frankie Bernstein was sitting at a corner table. Frankie loved clothes, especially his check jacket, black slacks, pink shirt and matching blue Italian silk tie. As an accountant he was offered a partnership in his uncle's auctioneer company. Harry Levine liked to keep business within the family, legitimate or otherwise. Following a gallstone operation, Harry is semi retired.

Frankie dovetailed his playboy lifestyle with his marriage, which never stood a chance. After five years of 'for better or worse' his wife filed for divorce. She got the Florida mansion, he kept the house in Minneapolis

St.Paul. In Frankie's words "the bitch got the kids *and* the sunshine!"

Elaine Mason appeared around nine, made her apologies, and sat down opposite. A combo played soft latin music. Frankie ordered cocktails as they studied the menu. Mason arranged the meeting. After her father died Frankie sold surplus family silver and Tiffany jewellery for Marcia, and advised on minor investments. He was more than useful. The waiter took their order.

'You look fantastic tonight, Elaine ; Bel Air suits you.'

'Forget the front Frankie, I'm in quicksand, up to my neck, and need help. It goes like this …I got involved in a Florida deal which curdled. Swamp land was cheap but as it was drained became very valuable. As you know, prices doubled and trebled overnight. You may recall a harbour was being developed that ran into Union trouble. Shipping blacklisted Miami and funding dried up. To get things moving, the developers invited another source to inject capital, who were linked to the Union. So far so good, but it fell short when those shysters got greedy and hatched a plot to sell the same land twice over to unsuspecting clients. As this was swamp, which took time to drain and couldn't be built on, there was a time lapse, just long enough for fraud to take place on a massive scale.'

'Sure, I heard rumours from several sources that got 'burned'. Did you know anything about this?'

'That's just it. My partner was involved and confessed all. He was in on the scam. Last week they dragged his car from a Miami swamp. He had been squelched by alligators, nothing left but his driver's licence. Hardly any use to those four legged 'meat grinders', unless you've seen one driving a car lately.'

'So call the Cops.'

'And prove what? They have his death down as a suicide.'

'Which means that someone is very uptight, believes you are implicated, and is looking for a refund, or worse still, a 'blood transfusion'.'

'My phone has been tapped, and as a frightener the fuel line on my aircraft severed. In my line of business, cemented to a studio contract, scandal is the last thing I need!'

'Slow down, Elaine'…

'Sure, and get buried. I need something fast to negotiate with. Come on Frankie, give me an option!'

Bernstein fingered his cocktail stick, ate the cherry, and placed it on a side plate before taking a long drink.

'So why not organise a 'pay off' and end it?'

'I already thought of that, or even disappear for a while. Maybe Canada, you can lose yourself up there, but I'm contracted to a studio who pay well. There is a little put aside, should they come calling, but not nearly enough. I don't want to end up as one of Vera Pilcher's crocodile handbags. There must be something on offer.'

Frankie, never short of an opportunity, or angle, tried to mix business with a little pleasure.

'You know I've always liked you Elaine, perhaps when this mess is over we could spend some precious time together.'

'Sure Frankie, let's hit Casablanca and I'll play the part of Bergman. Get on with what you have in mind.' He waited for the meal to be served, and out of earshot, outlined a way out.

'It goes like this. We could use Thursday's auction. It's a syndicate operation. They won't know you are acting alone, I'll take care of that. It's an auction of sapphires. Not your ordinary ones that you pay a markup for at your local jewellers, these are *pink* sapphires at this unique sale.' 'So what's so special about pink sapphires?'

'Simply the price and future demand. Look at it this way. Quality diamonds are already way too expensive for most folk and will soon be beyond the reach of ladies wanting engagement rings. There will always be demand for second rate gems because most buyers can't see the difference, but, at the top end of the market, those seeking pink diamond engagement rings will soon turn to pink sapphires as a great alternative They are beautiful, natural gemstones, and come in colours ranging from pale pinks to almost red. It may surprise you that some ladies consider them more appealing. The rare stones already fetch a higher price than normal blue sapphires. Pink ones are known as *gems from heaven* and come at basement prices.'

'Are you sure I can handle it Frankie? I'm new to all of this.'

'Sure you can. Get ahead of the market. You will make an instant profit on your purchase. These are top quality three carat cut and uncut stones from Madagascar. Your Hollywood friends will love them.

Come prepared to settle on the day. That's all you need to know. We'll finalise any details Thursday.'

Frankie called over the waiter and paid the bill. He declined a lift home in her cream Packard.

Blue Sails

Wednesday morning Nick Carter rose early and entered the kitchen for breakfast. He could smell the bacon, or 'ham' as they liked to call it, cooking on the griddle, organised by Mae the cook. She glanced up from her busy schedule. 'If you are looking for Caroline she's already out.'

So soon, he thought, *what time do these people rise around here?* He grabbed a slice of toast, added an apple, and left by the kitchen door in a hurry. Caroline's Westie called 'Phyl' followed him outside down to the lake.

'You might catch her at the barn,' Mae shouted, 'that's where she keeps her boat…what about this ham and eggs?'

Nick was gone, but felt guilty and apologetic. The

previous evening Caroline had mentioned a mornings sailing. He was keen then, all ready to set sail, but here he was, running late as usual.

The barn was large and so old it may have preceded the house. The bleached wood sides supported a pitched roof. Over time wild honeysuckle had grown up one side and partially covered the shingle cladding. Even at that early hour the blossom provided a lovely sweet scent. A grey squirrel leapt from the roof into the top of a nearby birch. Caroline, dressed in waterproofs over a sweater struggled to open the second large door. Nick approached and offered help. With both doors open he looked inside.

'She's beautiful,' he said.

'And has blue sails.'

'No not the boat…I mean the car. This must be Elaine's Packard. It's enormous!'

He moved closer, took out his camera, squeezed past the boat and started to take photos. Caroline frowned.

'You can take one of me if you like.'

Nick stopped, and realised he had hurt her feelings.

'Sorry, we don't see these in England, and yes I like your boat.'

'Really, you mean that. She's an Enterprise, rare for these parts. Dad left Elaine the Packard, Mom bought me the boat and the horses.'

He tried a little charm. 'Can we take a look?'

'Maybe later, they're in the paddock. Let's get this craft in the water, it's a Club competition this morning and you are my crew.'

Nick had never sailed before but grabbed hold of the bow and, with her guidance, manoeuvred the boat downhill across the lawn and into the lake. Once in the water, it easily floated from the trailer. They waved farewell to little Phyl, who looked disappointed. On board, Caroline adjusted the drop keel, rigged the sail, secured their life jackets, and pushed off using a paddle. She grasped the rudder and headed *Tomahawk* to the start line at the far end of the lake near the Clubhouse. Other boats were already there with crews jostling for position.

'No time for photos, Nick. Stay alert. With these light winds, we won't capsize, but whatever happens the built-in airbags will keep her afloat. She's sturdy and designed in your part of the world. Those two guys over there are National Champions and know these waters. We'll track them. They taught me to sail, but

I haven't beaten them yet. Maybe today! Take the stop watch, set it by the ten minute gun and countdown to me at three minutes. The start line is between those two points off shore.'

Nick pretended to take it all in as crews competed for space and position. The Champions prematurely crossed the line so had to turn back and restart. There was a lot of shouting and debate. Meanwhile Caroline stayed focussed, took advantage of the chaos, chose a good slot and found herself in the lead position. It was all about seeking out the wind and tactics. She constantly checked the small triangular flag attached to a wire at the mast head for wind speed and direction.

It was a good start, better than expected with a scratch crew. They rounded the first mark safely, with no other boats in contention. On the second reach a stiffening breeze enabled two boats to suddenly come from behind, which impeded *Tomahawk* when rounding the buoy. As they leveled, the front boat collided.

'Hands off Nick!' Caroline screamed… 'get your hands off the side of the boat!'

She anticipated the danger. It was all split second. Nick withdrew his right hand as the other boat crunched into the side of *Tomahawk*. He was shocked by the sudden impact and lucky escape, fell backwards on releasing his grip, and almost went overboard. Caroline struggled to grab his life jacket strap and haul him back into position. For a moment the boat stalled and the mainsail flapped, but it tightened as Caroline regained control. The incident cost them two places.

'Forget it Nick. The excitement is over, you're still playing piano!'

The remainder of the race passed without incident. Despite their false start, the Champions came fast along the final leg to claim second place. Caroline had to be content with fourth from an entry of twelve. The race over, they returned home.

'Better count your fingers, Nick,' she said with a smile… and he did!

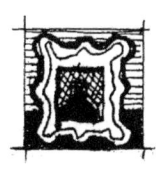

AUCTION
– NICK CARTER

Early Thursday morning, Elaine asked me to drive her into Minneapolis. Following the near loss of a limb on Caroline's boat, and being asked to drive the dream machine, you will understand my nerves were all over the place ; once behind the wheel I took on a new confidence, made sure we arrived in good time and navigated through busy urban traffic, despite all those 'other cars' being driven on the *wrong* side of the road! Elaine went inside the auction house, I stayed outside to keep an eye on the car.

No one paid much attention to the lady in the third row. A silk head scarf covered her blond hair, and large sunglasses disguised suntanned features. Her light-coloured Macintosh partially hid a pale blue dress. No one noticed that she made bids on every fourth lot. She was interested only in paintings, oils to be exact, with heavy ornate frames. A few newcomers to Levene's Auction House were surprised by the high prices offered, against keen competition, for what were unknown artists, but this was an auction, and strange things happen.

The auctioneer missed one of her bids on Lot 159 and sold it. Despite the gavel coming down she raised an objection and bidding restarted. This seemed unusual, but Bernstein apologised, ignored the protests, and second time around Mason outbid everyone to secure the Lot. Frankie's extra commission was safe.

Satisfied with five purchases, she discretely left the room, walked over to the office and paid the total sum by guaranteed cheque. One of the staff, in a dark green apron, carefully placed the paintings inside the waiting Packard. Elaine Mason was satisfied with her visit. I opened the car door for her.

'Thanks for waiting Nick. This calls for a celebration! Head for the Mimosa, Lakeside, and we'll have a spot of lunch, just the two of us.'

Elaine had me by the 'emotions'. In less than a week she had manoeuvred this south London boy into a position where, for a fleeting moment, I thought we were in love. I forgot she was an actress. To her, feelings were no more than dollars, cents and dimes. At first I believed she needed a helping hand. It made me feel good about myself. She let me drive her precious Packard. I loved that car. She trusted me with it. Whatever the doubts, they were submerged the moment I turned on the ignition, and heard the sound of that enormous engine. The reality was different as I fell headlong into a web of deceit while looking the other way.

* * *

Thursday night was special. Blame it on the Moet Champagne or "Balmy" Minnesota weather. Sitting on the porch we watched lightning flash across the lake. A sudden chill in a whisper of breeze signalled rain was heading our way. When it arrived we moved indoors. She placed both arms around my neck as we slowly moved to a latin beat.

'You were wonderful today, Nick. Will you take me for another drive soon?'

'Sure, when do you want to go?'

THE CREAM PACKARD

Our lips met for the first time.

'Take me now, Nick!'

'But it's way too wild out there.'

'I feel wild…don't you feel wild tonight, Nick Carter?'

'Better get your windcheater, you'll need to wrap up.'

'Forget the gear, bring the car around, I'll be waiting for you.'

I did as I was told and she ran across the drive and got into the cream Packard. Even over that short distance the downpour soaked her hair and bare shoulders. I set the ignition to start the engine.

'Anywhere special?' I enquired.

'Just drive Nick… drive!'

It was surreal. The car shot ahead as I pressed the accelerator to the floor. With no idea where we were heading, and in the dark, I quickly lost my bearings and got confused.

'There it is!' she screamed.

'What?' I said, searching the road for anything visible.

'The lightning Nick… follow the lightning!'

We tracked the storm a good five miles, following the outline of the lake. In one brief moment, I did wonder if there were any other fools in love enduring that same frenzy. Or should I make that a singular fool in love. As if not enough, Elaine leant over and turned on the radio at full blast. On cue …Jerry Lee Lewis's 'Whole lot of Shaking' came over loud and clear.

Along with Jerry Lee, I was shaking all right!

Don't recall much more of that crazy night. We slowed down and parked up at the far end of the lake as the storm died away. After all the excitement, Elaine leaned into my shoulder and fell asleep. I changed the radio station to catch the end of Dean Martin's 'That's Amore'. Somehow I managed to find our way back, carry her inside, and garage the car… honest I did!

Care Home
– Mary Christie

Mary Christie was the only daughter of wealthy French Canadian parents from Montreal. She met Warren Clarke at a Tennis tournament sponsored by her father's mining company. Following a brief engagement they married and honeymooned in Bermuda.

When her father died she inherited a portfolio of investments. The best of these included prime real estate throughout Florida. About the same time Clarke had fallen in 'lust' with a Swedish blond. By chance his latest squeeze (there had been others) was employed at a care home. By another coincidence of ill-fortune, it was around this time that Mary became unwell. With Mary out of the way, he inherited her fortune.

*　*　*

'I am confused, doctor, often depressed for no reason, and losing my memory. These sensations, when I feel the last breath leaving my body are the worst. Could these be anxiety attacks, they are dreadful?'

'Exactly when did these symptoms first occur?'

'About a month ago. They come and go, which is why I haven't felt the need to see you earlier.'

Dr. Tiselius examined his patient, reassured her that the symptoms were not serious, suggested she change her routine, take things easy for a while, and prescribed medication. Over the next two months her mental health rapidly deteriorated. Warren Clarke sought and bought a second opinion and Mary was quickly dispatched to a carefully selected care home. In medical speak, it was all too clinical. Joanne was distraught by her mothers illness and almost succumbed to her own breakdown. On her father's advice, visits to see her mother were curtailed.

Nobody came to see Mary. A snowball of lies ensured her identity was hidden. She was locked in a single room on her own, and sedated. There was only one key. When she eventually struggled across the floor and glimpsed in the mirror, she didn't recognise her own image. Her hair was cropped and dyed, her cheeks sunk through loss of weight. The nightmare lasted all of twelve months.

She is hazy about this, but recalls hearing a loud bell and being rushed and pushed along a long corridor. An illicit cigarette in one of the storage rooms probably triggered an alarm. For the first time she was placed among other patients. A young doctor was in attendance and introduced himself as Colby Jenssen. He asked her several questions, took notes, and called her 'Alice'. None of this registered with Mary. He moved away, but she thought there was something familiar about this young man. Perhaps she recognised his voice. As he left she was swiftly returned by wheelchair to her room. He had not recognised her. Had she altered that much? she wondered.

Mary can't recall when she stopped taking the tablets that were slowly destroying her, but it followed soon after the doctor's visit. A nurse regularly checked the doses and knew all the hiding places. To avert further suspicion she was allowed into the Art Class, which provided an opportunity to dispose of them. Each pill was crushed and fed into empty paint tubes.

The ends were rolled up to the cap and discarded. The hardest part was crushing the tablets so she placed them under one of the bed ends and bounced up and down on the mattress. It was fun for a while. She faked sedation by sleeping most of the day.

There was no obvious means of escape so Mary hatched a plot and complained of severe toothache, adding an abscess to compound the problem and speed up attention. A couple of days later an ambulance arrived. Accompanied by a male nurse, she was taken to a local surgery and seated in a dentists chair. The nurse left the room as the dentist pressed a lever which sent the chair backwards in a jerk that made her head spin.

'What seems to be the problem?' he enquired. Mary found it difficult to get the words out.

'Nothing wrong with my teeth, just get me out of here!'

'Did you say there was an abscess? There's no need to be nervous, it's normal.'

'Nothing's 'normal' you idiot, call the Cops, I've been kidnapped!'

He pressed the lever in reverse and the chair recoiled to the normal position, giving her another jolt.

'Better get in here Karl,' he called out. 'We've got another one. Wants me to call the Cops. Poor soul, take her back, that's the third one this month!'

On her return, she feigned sickness. The nurse jumped into the ambulance for a bowl. In that moment, Mary threw an envelope under the vehicle and prayed someone would find it. The letter was addressed to Vera Pilcher.

BASEBALL

Around five o'clock Thursday evening, Barbara and Matt sat either side of a small corner table at the Drugstore. Shelli appeared wearing her neat check uniform and trade white shoes.

'You two are becoming regulars, what'll it be this time?'

'Two coffees and he'll have a doughnut.'

'Regular or large?'

Johnson looked up from the menu. 'Gee, do they come in different sizes?'

'She means the coffee you dope… make it two large.'

Hogarth took out a notepad as Johnson opened the conversation.

'Have you heard of Lottie Bumblebee and the Four Stingers?'

'Sure, they're big in LA, a regular slot on the Jonny Carson Show, Saturdays.'

'How come I've never heard of them, I thought I knew all the rock groups. Must be a European import. I'll have to ask that kid from London – what's his name? – Nick, he'll know.'

Hogarth smiled. 'Who have you been talking to? For sure Nick won't know.'

'I bumped into Caroline as she was leaving the Doctor's Surgery.'

'That explains it! You must have hurt her feelings again. She thinks you are a clown. "Lottie Bumblebee" is street talk for "buzz off", get lost!'

Johnson didn't see the funny side.

'You need more brain food. Lay off Dairy Queen for a while,' she added.

* * *

As a regular reporter, insults to Matt Johnson were like injuries during a boxing match... unavoidable. Some you get over, others linger a while. He regained what was left of his ego and placed two tickets on the table.

'My, you are full of surprises. Are you taking me to the Ball, kind sir?'

'In a manner of speaking, yes. We are invited to the game tonight. The Senators are playing St.Louis Cardinals in an exhibition match.'

'Don't tell me you already paid for these, I might have another date,' she teased.

'The choice is yours. Vera Pilcher sent them over. It turns out she owns the team and will be more disappointed than me if you don't show.'

'Sounds like a Royal Command so I had better say "yes", but I've a hunch Vera will want payback.'

* * *

They arrived at the impressive Metropolitan Stadium around seven, were escorted to a private box, and waited for Vera.

'She's probably in the changing room applying the liniment.' 'Or doing a spot of ironing,' she replied dryly.

The box provided a spectacular view of the floodlit pitch where the players were already out limbering up. Several favourites stood by the low boundary rail signing autographs for young fans who had rushed

THE CREAM PACKARD

down the stadium steps to meet them. One or two signed programmes and baseballs as mementos. A group of attendants in immaculate white uniforms were busy sorting hamburgers and ice cream for the interval. Hogarth surveyed the scene. It was her first match.

'Are they the teams, they look like giants?'

'And they get giant money. Should the ball come our way, be sure to catch it and keep it as a souvenir.'

'If it does, you had better pass me one of those large leather gloves, I forgot to bring my shopping bag!'

Vera joined them with a couple more guests just before the first 'pitch'. The game started slowly with neither side scoring. The local team was in good form early on, but, despite several huge strikes into the outfield, made no progress.

As happens in baseball, the Cardinals Pitcher lost a little magic and the Senators went ahead by one. In the second innings the Cardinals 'star' player hit a couple behind the receiver then struck a huge hit left side. Two players went for the catch but collided. Somehow the ball struck one player on the upper body. It bounced sideways and fell into the gloved hand of the player lying outstretched on his back. The crowd loved it!

The Senators were ahead into the third game but never finished. Dark clouds suddenly developed into torrential rain and the game was abandoned. Vera apologised to her guests.

' I can arrange most things, even 'fix' a match, but the almighty has the last word on the weather. Let me make it up to you. Stop by later for drinks, you know where I live.'

* * *

With little to do on a wet night, they accepted the impromptu invitation and an hour later arrived outside Vera's house. It was a prime piece of real estate constructed in natural stone with brick panels either side of the main doorway. Large terra cotta pots, oozing a kaleidoscope of colourful 'impatiens' complemented an impressive entrance. Vera came to the front door.

'Maid's night off, but we'll do our best.'

She flew into a rage when she glanced at her car parked outside the garage.

'Bloody driver has left the hood down. After all that rain, it will be a swimming pool inside!'

They entered and Hogarth was impressed by

the lavish interior. All soft pastel shades in creams, whites and yellows. Imported French silk drapes complimented the outsized windows. Following dry martinis there was no small talk from Vera. She showed them the letter.

'The handwriting is shaky but there is no doubt in my mind it is from Mary Christie. We used to correspond regularly when organising charity events. She always signed her letters "MC". This one has a single letter "M", probably to avoid detection. It sounds frantic, but has no address or contact number.'

Hogarth examined the contents.

'Has anyone else seen this?'

'God no, and especially not Warren Clarke.'

'What about the Police?'

'An obvious choice, but, if she is incarcerated some place, there are no limits to the number of people implicated or bribed.'

'Did you ask Joanne?' Johnson enquired.

'The short answer is no, I did not. I am worried for Mary. If Clarke gets a hint that I am trying to trace her he may change locations overnight. If that happens she will be lost forever. The envelope has a local postmark so she must be nearby. To some, this information would mean a lot of money. Even a private dick would work both ends against the middle of this charade.'

'So why put your faith in us?'

'Several reasons, take your pick. There may be a good headline here which could flush out any wrongdoing. The authorities would take notice. Most importantly, you can move around and make discreet enquiries, without arousing suspicion. Last, but not least, Barbara will keep you in line, Matt. Won't you my dear?'

Johnson took the letter and carefully placed it in his pocket.

' We share your concern. It would make good copy, but let's not jump to conclusions. First we have to find her whereabouts, and determine if she is still alive. For now keep this conversation private and we will be in touch.'

Outside it had stopped raining but turned cold as he switched on the ignition and lights to the Station Wagon.

'That was a fabulous car, we saw tonight.'

'Sure was,' he replied. 'All extras, including a flooding option!'

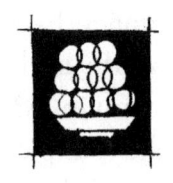

Care Home
– From Here to Eternity

It was a long shot, but one worth taking. Vera's precious letter had an Excelsior postmark. There were three nearby care homes. One had been closed last week for irregularities. A second was owned by the state, but the third was private and very discreet.

'Try discreet,' Hogarth suggested.

Friday morning Johnson approached Oakwood on foot after leaving his car further along the drive. It was an old stone building with a mass of ivy clawing it's way into the eves of one wing. He announced his arrival and a young girl invited him inside.

'I represent 'From Here To Eternity'. We are funeral directors, new to the County, and would like to offer our services…at modest rates, you understand.'

The girl looked surprised.

'My you *are* quick. Mrs.Swinhufuud only passed away ten minutes ago. The Director will be impressed!'

'Have one of my cards,' he said, thrusting it into her hand. Again she looked puzzled.

'There is nothing on this. Is this some kind of joke?'

'Pardon me ma'am, at 'Eternity' we believe death is a serious business, and treat 'stiffs', I mean the deceased, as a priority.'

He grabbed the card from her and added his bookmaker's phone number.

'Life's a gamble. Ring that number whenever you need us.' She removed her spectacles and ushered him into an office.

'Wait here please, you will need a 'death certificate'. Would you like coffee?'

Johnson declined, sat down, and drew a packet of cigarettes from his pocket. She looked up from her typing.

'We have a no smoking rule here. It's bad for your health.'

Ironic he thought, a non smoking policy in a "living morgue". After twenty minutes Colby Jenssen arrived.

'Gee, don't I know you, Doc. I was at your wedding last weekend. Short honeymoon?'

'Sort of, we are going away later but, for now, we are renovating our new home. What is the name of your firm?'

'From Here To Eternity'. Catchy ain't it? Did you see the film? Wasn't Deborah Kerr just great. But they should have added a couple more lobsters to that famous beach scene with Lancaster.' He kept talking and gambled that Jenssen never knew he was a reporter.

'You have a swell setup here Doc. Bet you keep the old folks happy.'

'We cater for a wide range of patients of all ages. I was on my way to the art class, it's one of our more interesting activities. Come with me.' They moved a short distance along the corridor.

'Been here long Doc?'

'I am not resident; I only attend as and when needed, it works out about weekly.'

They entered the studio through a half open door.

'Please speak slowly if you have to. They enjoy wonderful freedom in the art class. Take Oscar… only last week he was shredding bed sheets and trying to abscond every Friday night. It was a mystery the staff couldn't figure out until we learnt that Swedish Meatballs were on the menu at the local Drugstore. We've added meatballs to Friday's lunch menu and introduced Oscar to more creative thinking. He's settled now, but still frisky.'

'Smart move Doc, but you are way ahead of me. What is the connection between Oscar's cravings and art?'

'Good question, but a simple answer. We get Oscar to paint meatballs all week long. Not just any, you understand, but fat juicy prime beef examples.'

'Won't he fancy a nibble if they are on a plate out there?'

'Briefly no. We provide colour photos to copy from. Mind you, early on we had life-like models of meatballs for him to paint from. They were made of clay.'

'That was more realistic?' said Johnson.

'It was, until one day the smell of fried onions came into the studio from the canteen. It was too much for Oscar.'

'So what happened?'

'He started eating the clay meatballs!'

'Was that so bad?'

'No, but we had a near riot on our hands. The

other residents felt cheated. We had to lay on extra hamburgers and anything else Cook could muster that night just to keep the peace!'

'That's the genius of Psychiatry,' quipped Johnson. 'Who would have thought meatballs would come between a man and his emotions?'

* * *

The group had seven residents sat behind easels. A bowl of fruit placed on a table provided the subject. Johnson was curious and moved slowly around the room. The first few sketches revealed a contrast in style. Nothing unusual there, but one effort portrayed a house. He turned to the doctor.

'Doesn't she like fruit?'

'She always paints an image of a blue house with peculiar fencing.'

Johnson got no further. The door opened and the Director walked in. She introduced herself as Dr.Britt Lisell.

'What have they been showing you Mr.Johnson? We can't waste any more of your precious time, especially with a body to dispose of.'

He made a hasty retreat.

'Thank you all, I'll send the hearse around within the hour.'

The Death Certificate was left behind as he returned to the car where Hogarth was waiting.

'What kept you? I've almost finished the crossword. Listen up…last clue, seven letters, a person who enjoys food and drink?'

'Try "glutton".'

'Nice try, but wrong. It has to be "epicure".'

'Are you sure? That sounds more like a laxative to me.'

'Speaking of strange, any signs of Mary Christie?'

'Well, there are two surprises. An odd - looking lady, but without a photo I can't be sure. She had this obsession with a blue house and peculiar fencing.'

'Like the type you described earlier?'

'The same.'

'That fencing could be all over Hennepin County.'

'No, it's rare, you don't often see it anymore. Look at it this way, if we can find a house like that, close by, with that fencing, and it turns out to be Warren Clarke's former home, then that poor soul in there is Mary Christie or the former Mrs.Mary Clarke. Here's

THE CREAM PACKARD

another for your notepad. Colby Jenssen is the resident Doctor!'

'Surely, he spotted his mother in law.'

'That bit I can't figure out. Maybe he's part of it. I almost asked him if he recognised Mary, but they could have whisked her away!'

The Blue House

Late Friday afternoon, they took a walk to the nearest Real Estate office. It was Hogarth's idea. Earlier she phoned Vera Pilcher to find the house location. No joy there. All correspondence was mailed to a charity office in Minneapolis, but she thought the house was on the lake.

A young man came from behind a desk. He was tall, and smartly dressed in a grey lightweight suit with a polkadot bow tie. He introduced himself.

'Good afternoon, I'm Chris Starren. Are you buying today?'

It was a direct approach, but not unusual for those parts.

'Show us some prime Real Estate around the lake,' Hogarth demanded.

He pointed to a couple of photos pinned to a board on the wall of the office but she feigned disappointment.

'Anything more upmarket? The best homes have their own jetties. Is the Clarke house for sale?'

'Sorry ma'am, don't recall that name. Prime property rarely comes onto the market. You could try Hillcrest, further along, but they are closed today, family bereavement.'

It wasn't clear who decided the next move, but they guessed the Blue House was on the east shoreline. She reckoned it was more exciting searching in a speed boat than wading through property records.

'Pay the man and make sure there is a reverse on this thing, we don't want to get stranded!'

Johnson took further instruction from the attendant who released the mooring. They set off, slowly at first, until he increased the speed of the Curtis 20, once clear of the shore. It was a sluggish departure from a neglected boat.

Large detached wooden built houses lay along the waters edge, separated by thickets of familiar birch, alder and maple. The lake was quiet, almost deserted, except for several mothers and daughters fishing in the shallows. Some dwellings were weekend retreats.

'This house may be difficult to find,' he said.

'Then take a short cut. Ask that kid over there on that jetty. He must live nearby.'

Johnson swung the boat into an arc and pulled alongside, carefully avoiding the outstretched fishing line.

'Caught any?'

'Only Sunfish, been a poor year, too much pollution.'

'We are looking for the Clarke house, maybe painted blue.'

'Means little to me, but if you are buying, there's one for sale at the end of the lake. Somebody was here yesterday. Don't know who lived there but they had a daughter. She often water-skied and scared the fish. Never got a bite when she was around!'

Johnson turned the boat back into the lake and headed to what looked like a boathouse, where they got out. A winding path through tall grass and reeds took them further inshore. The sun had almost disappeared when they got their first glimpse of a large residence which was painted blue.

Two cars were parked outside the main entrance. A man was loading what looked like rectangular

THE CREAM PACKARD

wrapped packages into a juniper green Chevrolet pickup, hardly visible against dense vegetation in the fading light. He carefully covered the goods with a plastic sheet and secured it all with a rope. A heated argument developed with a lady who abruptly got into a cream Packard and drove off. They recognised the man. It was Warren Clarke.

'Did you get a shot of that?' he asked.

'In this light, and at this range, are you kidding? I'm freezing, should have worn a sweater, it's always cold near water. I don't see any of your historic fencing, but it's a blue house. It ain't fair. One guy has all this, then marries a wealthy widow.'

'Show me fair, and I'll tell you it's stopped raining,' he replied.

'I guess that clinches it. Mary is alive and this is her home. We'll confirm this to Vera. Was that Elaine Mason with Clarke? What was she doing here tonight?'

'You saw the Packard didn't you, it had to be her,' he replied.

The Cream Packard

Everything settled into place Friday morning after the storm. The lake took on a freshness as small groups of black moorhen busily worked their way in and around dense reeds at the waters edge. Giant Monarch Butterflies drifted into bright early sunshine. Several grey squirrels clawed their way up the sides of the barn as Nick opened the large wooden doors. His memory of Croydon, ravaged by flying bombs and deadly land mines was fading fast.

He entered and began to remove five pictures purchased at the auction. An elderly man, in faded blue denim, wearing an old wide – brimmed straw hat, frayed at the edges, approached.

'You must be Nick, heard all about you.'

Nick shook the outstretched hand.

'Call me Josh. I'm the handyman around here. Ain't she a beauty?'

'Sure is,' Nick replied. 'Tell me about her.'

'Been in the family a while, and bought by Mr. Mason. Belongs to Elaine now. This particular model is a 1935 Packard 1207 convertible Coup Roadster, with all the original coachwork, including the crimson leather interior and matching carpet. I heard Brad Mason say it once belonged to a famous film star from Los Angeles. It's a Packard V12 and boy is she powerful, with 175 BHP, a three speed manual transmission, and servo assisted drum brakes, with adjustable shock absorbers. This car is well known in the American automobile industry and was one of the last to be completed by Ray Dietrich, a famous designer at that time. I reckon it was the best of the bunch. A classic amongst classics.'

'Why such a large engine?'

'Back then new highways were under construction. People traveled further, coast to coast. This engine provided a desire for more speed, more smoothness, more power. V12 engines had already been used in aircraft, speedboats, and racing cars… but Packard were the first to introduce a V12 production car. It was some achievement!'

'You're from England, aren't you? Well this will interest you. As part of the war effort Packard built aircraft engines. They licensed the famous Merlin engine from Rolls Royce to produce the V-1650 which powered the Mustang fighter and gave us the edge over enemy aircraft at that time. There were later and bigger models like the impressive Darrin and Lincoln Continental, but there has never been a car like this.

Take a closer look at the features, Nick. The rumble seat at the rear, and the golf bag door, cleverly slotted into the bodywork, in case you fancy a game. You can play with the radio later, there are some good local stations. Honestly, did you ever see chrome work like that?'

'Have you looked after her over the years Josh?'

'Sure... Mae reckons I spend more time in the barn than with her.'

'So you two are married?'

'These last thirty years. It's getting to be a habit. We came from Mexico and worked for the Masons at their holiday home in Monterey. When they sold up we moved here with them. Minnesota winters are the worst, but we get by.'

Nick moved to the drivers side.

'I love those crazy white wall tyres, never seen that before.'

'You into cars, Nick?'

'I'm no mechanic, it's the styling, colours and finishes that intrigue me, all packaged in chrome. You sure have taken care of her. Elaine let me drive yesterday, but I was nervous.'

'Hell you are lucky. I only get to back this beauty out of the barn once in a while to wash her down. The cover never keeps all the dust off. Have you seen the engine?'

'Only a glimpse before we set off. It's enormous, like everything else over here. Maybe you can explain more later after I get through unpacking. Elaine wants a picture delivered to her aircraft on the lake. She says I have to take special care with the ornate frame as they are delicate and valuable.'

* * *

Early Saturday morning Nick was disturbed by a loud noise. His room was small, previously used by one of the maids. It overlooked the lake. A dog barked. His right hand moved the alarm clock closer. The time was ten past five, almost too early for birdsong. Slowly he emerged from bed, covered his bare torso with a gown, then moved to the window. The sound became more regulated, then increased. It was the sound of an aircraft engine.

What followed was a high pitched whine as Mason's Cessna sped across the large expanse of water and lifted into the sky behind a group of pine trees. *She's gone*, he thought, *and not even a goodbye*!

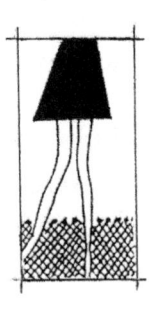

Pink Sapphires
– Murky and Bimbo

After a one hour flight, early Saturday, Elaine Mason landed at a remote lake west of Chicago. All was quiet, the place looked deserted, the only movement coming from an overhead orange aviation windsock attached to a wood pole. She squeezed out of the cockpit and slowly walked to the end of a disused jetty.

At a distance a car approached at speed, smothered in a cloud of dust. She removed her aviator sunglasses, loosened the white silk scarf around her neck, and waited. As it drew closer the chrome of the 1954 Buick Wildcat dream car in metallic blue reflected the early sunlight from a cloudless sky. The car came alongside and stopped. A young lady got out. She walked towards Mason and, without introduction, began to speak.

'I saw you come in. Do you pilot that thing by yourself? Heard so much about you, even seen one of your movies.'

Mason slowed the tempo.

'If you are nice to me you might get an autograph, or, better still, you can drive me. So where's the midget. Have you left him in the glove box?'

'The gimp don't like being called small.'

'He's been called worse. Where is he? I was expecting a parade.'

'At the motel. Have you got the package?'

Mason pointed to the aircraft and got into the car. The girl collected the picture and struggled back to place it inside the boot. She slid into the drivers seat, turned the ignition, and moved away. Ten minutes later the car was parked and Mason entered a room where two men waited. The smaller of the two rose from his chair. She could taste the evil from this man.

Murky, original name Murphy, was short, fat and muscular. A product of Irish immigrants, his early years were spent as a fairground boxer who had moved into the 'pro' game after a hike from the Merelli mob. He was known to take more than the odd dive, which pleased his benefactors. Following on, he worked as a muscle man for Joe Bronitski in Jersey. Murky had a laconic sense of humour. When Joe was found floating face down in the Chesapeake, it was Murky who remarked that "he should have been wearing a life jacket!"

Some say he fractured his left leg kicking poor Joe to death, but it was more likely it happened when he fell onto the tracks after a train heist out of Chicago. Despite a poor start, he learned fast, and against all odds moved ahead.

The other man was taller and slimmer. Dressed in a well-cut black suit he looked "carbon copy business". She guessed he was hired short term for his expertise. The scene reminded her altogether of a cheap gangster film set, complemented by the scantily clad girl she met earlier, who sat in a shady corner of the room. Carla Santiago was her name. She possessed a coffee complexion and ultra slim figure. Her long, bare, smooth legs went on to infinity, with a black skirt to match, which travelled in the opposite direction. She had full lips, like an inflated inner tube, and dark piercing eyes. She was Murky's moll and he called her "Bimbo".

Carla Santiago was born in Cuba. Her mother left

that troubled island with her two daughters in 1939 and never returned. Her sister was called Zamira. Their father remained to work in a local cigar factory and from time to time sent a few dollars subsistence. Even this meagre amount terminated when he joined Che Guevara's guerrillas against Fulgencio Batista and was killed in action attacking a Police Station.

Desperate, her mother sought domestic work in Florida. They moved around a lot. Carla left school on her fourteenth birthday and began work as a waitress. She drifted into singing in small bars around Miami.

For a while she lived with Johnny Salago who owned the Barracuda Club in Hammarshee, but when Johnny got a seven stretch for narcotic violation with his Cuban friends, and spent time at Noma Road, she left. Carla acted as interpreter for the Cuban connection, but nothing was ever proven by the local Law Enforcement. Some say she turned States evidence and got paid. Either way, with Johnny gone, she sold the Barracuda for a quick profit , and made an even quicker exit.

Carla moved on to the Flamingo Club in Fort Lauderdale, under an assumed name, where she met Murky. He had funded Salago's first venture into

Cuba, but they fell out. They say Murky "extinguished" Salago the same day he was released from prison... so all that parole he accumulated came to sweet nothing. The Law was grateful to be rid of Salago. No charges were pressed. Off - duty cops were familiar faces at the Flamingo for a while after that. Meanwhile, Murky was so busy "eyeballing" Carla's long legs, he never caught on that she had "shafted" him by selling the Barracuda.

Later they both left for Chicago, but she never got used to the cold climate and persuaded Murky to buy a villa in Florida where she stayed most of the time. As it turned out, Murky's extortion racket turned sour when the Puerto Rican crews moved in. He was forced into developing other lines of business and considered a permanent move to Florida.

To close it off, Carla Santiago persuaded Murky that extortion was no longer viable : too violent, too dangerous and too costly. Even the victims began demanding discounts and luncheon vouchers! She saw narcotics as the new Eldorado in 1947 and persuaded "lover boy" to restart where Salago had left off.

Pink Sapphires
– The Deal

'Mr. Murphy, how nice to meet you in person, after all those pernicious threats.'

'Just make it Murky, everyone else does. No harm meant, sometimes my boys get over excited ; it's not every day they deal with, or should I say encounter, a real live tinsel queen. May I call you Elaine?'

Mason was impressed by the neatly tailored Italian navy suit, white shirt, silk tie and patent leather black shoes. It was all unexpected.

'This is Fredericks… he'll take a look at the sapphires, if that is all right with you.'

'Sure', she replied, 'but don't get ahead of yourself. This is a one off deal that brings everything level. There are no comebacks. As I explained on the phone, my business partner was responsible for your mess in Florida, he told me as much. Don't forget, I got dragged into this, and was only an investor like you.'

Murky slowly lit one of his favourite Cabras Cuban cigars.

'Look at it from my side. We took a massive hit. Almost wiped me out, and others who came in with me. I don't want to see my dough devoured by a swamp in Florida. Resurrect this deal and we can all move on. You won't walk away from this without my say so.' Mason felt the 'heat'.

'So level with me...who killed Cordola? was it you?'

A thin smile came from Murky.

'That's a tricky one... It could have been any one of a thousand 'alligators', each one with a watertight alibi. The guy had it coming. A lot of people got burned!'

* * *

Despite mincing the land deal without her knowledge, Mason reckoned her partner must have had his reasons. She had been fond of Andre Cordola, they had been close. Up to that point he had treated her well. For a while all had been "honey", and the house, pool, and sixty foot Ketch which he had named *Midnight Lady*, all part of it. They often sailed across to taste the magic of Havana. Long dreamy weekends. She detested this maggot in front of her and reckoned payback long overdue.

* * *

A waiter brought a trolley into the room.

'Forgive me, Elaine, I'm a poor host. Join us for drinks and some breakfast. That was quite a flight this morning. I'm impressed.'

She declined the alcohol, but sampled the scrambled eggs, caviar, and black coffee. From the outset she guessed Murky would pull a double cross, so planned for any shortfall. He was more sophisticated than she had imagined, but sentiment was never going to play any part of this arrangement. Fredericks made his apologies and moved to leave the room.

'You will find the gems in the corner of the picture frame, on the reverse side. The picture and valuable ornate frame, plus the gems makes a high valuation. I have the paperwork.'

THE CREAM PACKARD

Fredericks returned with the saphires and carefully placed them onto a velvet cloth. He produced an eyeglass to examine them. Even in that dim light, the stones sparkled. He called Murky over to the table. There was a heated exchange. 'Fredericks says there is a problem. His valuation falls way short of what you owe me. He reckons you are ten thousand light!'

This was a critical point in the deal and Mason had no intention of handing over one cent more than her limit. She cleverly withheld four paintings that covered the debt. It would take some acting.

Murky thought otherwise. *What was this dame up to? She must think I'm brain dead. Bet she didn't count on me having an on the spot valuer. Smart move. I've caught this dumb broad out. Let's put the bite on her, but gently.*

'I don't know what to say Mr. Murphy'...*please, it's Murky,* 'where can I get that sort of cash?'

'Well think about it…famous actress from Bel Air, there must be a little gravy there somewhere.'

'Let me mull this over, I need time.'

She sensed a sudden change.

'Sure … no sweat, take all of the next five minutes, you ain't going nowhere.'

Mason pleaded a while longer…… even discussed options, but knew none were viable.

'There is one solution, which will make you rich. I was going to use it as a pension, but guess this has blown that idea.'

'Tell me about it.'

'A guy I know bought a painting at the auction. He believes it to be the work of an obscure Italian. In fact it is a genuine Caravaggio, who is one of Italy's greatest sixteenth century masters.'

'How come I never heard of him?'

'Not many have. He never shot pool, and is not well known like Rembrandt or Canaletto. He was a rebel, a bit like you Murky, only more talented.'

'Bet he died broke, like most of those jerks. Well I don't intend to. Tell me more.'

'He knows less about painting than you do, so I'll advise him it's a poor investment which should be sold on to a private investor.'

Fredericks had been quiet but cut in with the obvious.

'All this sounds plausible, but how did you discover the true value of this work?'

'The auctioneer is a friend and confided there

had been a gigantic mistake when his art expert was off sick. Bernstein is trying to retrieve it without arousing suspicion. So get a move on Murky, you have competition. Every museum will offer megabucks for it. Dump the Buick, think Cadillac!'

Fredericks looked perplexed.

'I don't like the sound of this.'

'Nobody asked your opinion. You are here to value the rocks, period.'

Mason gave an inner sigh of relief. Her plan was moving as hoped but there were a few loose ends.

'You will have to collect the Caravaggio. I'm not delivering so you lot can whack me. Be nice to me for a change and I will be in touch soon to arrange the exchange.' She left the gems on the table and reckoned it was worth the price to buy some precious time.

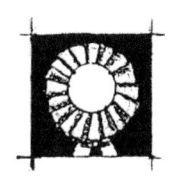

State Fair

Elaine Mason borrowed Marcia's car for easy parking at the stadium. Nick was at the wheel of the silver two-tone 1952 six cylinder Aero Willys sedan as they drove along route 494. On Saturday night, roads into the fair were busy, and traffic slow. Local kids rented back lots for parking spaces, so they left the car and walked a short distance to the main entrance.

It was hot, dusty and crowded. Everything was smothered in red, white and blue bunting. Mason felt tired after her return flight. Nick cheered up, and discretely avoided any awkward questions. They collected a double ticket, courtesy of Caroline, and climbed the steep steps into the arena. The Rodeo started, and the first flag waving riders, in stetsons, entered to a tumultuous Minnesota welcome. Caroline was not there. A spectator handed Mason an envelope.

'If you are Elaine, this note is for you. It was left on your seat.'

She thanked the lady, broke the seal, and read the note which said 'retrace your steps to a stable marked "Waxwing".' She left Nick to watch the show and walked along a deserted corridor beneath the main stand, past stables hung with polished bridles and saddles. Some walls were decorated with coloured rosettes.

Caroline had both arms around a chestnut stallion with blonde mane. Without looking up she spoke.

'Remember the first horse we used to share. Well this is her grandson. He's a beauty and entered for this evenings event. We have high hopes of him taking the Blue Riband.'

'Are you riding him?'

'Not tonight, the doctor says I have to take things easy for a while. Julie will take him round, she'll do a good job.'

'Well, I wish you every luck in the world Caroline, and hope you take that prize tonight.'

'Yes, it's about time some came my way. You cornered the market in luck Elaine... a college education, astute business connections, and now a movie star. What more is there?'

Mason always felt uneasy with her sisters mood swings. It was an almighty shock when she was diagnosed with depression following her eighteenth birthday. Maybe her father's sudden death triggered the illness, for that is what it was. She never understood the complexities, but, unknown to Caroline, paid the medical bills in the hope that a cure might be found.

'We all love you Caroline. Come back into the arena with me, Nick is here and would love to see you.'

She sensed the icy change in her sister and returned alone, but never allowed herself to enjoy the remainder of the Rodeo.

Double Cross

Saturday night, shortly after nine, Caroline phoned Britt Lisell from the State Fair. She was frantic.

'I know it's bloody inconvenient, but I have to see you... damn it you're my shrink!'

Lisell acquiesced and told her to drive over at ten. Friends leaving the stadium early gave Caroline a lift home, whereupon she grabbed her sister's car keys, removed the Packard from the barn, and drove across town to keep the appointment. Lisell was experienced in dealing with difficult patients. What happened on that night was unexpected and overwhelming. She left the annex door open for her patient to burst in shortly after ten thirty.

'Sit down, Caroline. Let me get you something.'

'Keep your distance witch, you've drugged me up

to the eyeballs. I'm a wreck. Are you trying to kill me?'

'It's an emotion, it will pass,' said Lisell.

'We are not talking bowel movements. It's my life, you've messed me up!'

'Leave this to me, it's a normal reaction to your tablets. I'll change your medication and you will feel better in the morning. Stay here tonight if you wish.'

Caroline became more animated.

'You don't get it, do you? It's not the bloody pills, it's your affair with Warren Clarke I'm talking about. Explain that!'

Lisell turned away, anxious to hide her sudden acute embarrassment. This was complex. Did Caroline know everything?

'It was no affair,' she lied. 'We are old friends from way back,' was her best excuse.

'More like friends from flat on your back. You are evil. I trusted you. Warren and I were going away together. It was all planned!'

'I can't deal with you when you are like this Caroline. All this is too personal. Let's fix an appointment for tomorrow.'

Caroline gave her a piercing glance. Her eyes were on fire. Drained of emotion, her voice became incoherent.

She got up slowly, went outside, struggled into the Packard, and left.

With Caroline gone, Lisell nervously lit a cigarette and poured herself a double vodka. Situation volatile! She had to act fast. Without clarifying her thoughts, she pushed her unfinished drink to one side, pulled on a sweater, rushed into her raven black 1955 Ford Thunderbird and headed towards the lake in the hope that her patient would follow the shoreline home. After a short distance, she was surprised to see an abandoned car with the door open.

Lisell braked suddenly and her tyres slid into loose gravel. She leapt out. The headlights revealed nothing. Suddenly, there was a scream. Without a torch, she followed the waters edge to a jetty that was silhouetted against the skyline, and then climbed onto it.

All was quiet now. She ran back and forth but saw nothing.It was only when she stepped off that a body appeared. It had drifted and wedged under the woodwork. Lisell waded into the cold water that came up to her waist, and pulled Caroline onto the grassy bank. She was dead. What happened next was not carefully planned.

She liked Caroline. Once they had been close.

Her first riding lesson was arranged by her as she was introduced to Waxwing. She always seemed happy around horses. Warren Clarke had tricked them both!

Lisell dragged and half carried the corpse into the boot of her car. A short drive along a track revealed a farm outbuilding where she opened the door to a granary and left the body inside. A dog barked. In blind panic, completely exhausted, she returned to the comfort of her car and quickly drove away.

In the madness of that moment, Lisell had committed a felony. The plan was to implicate her "lover" in the death of his step daughter, so an anonymous note was typed, and dropped into the Police Station letterbox. It detailed the crime scene. Early Sunday, the car boot was vigorously cleaned and all her wet clothes discarded. At that point, Lisell questioned her own actions. Blind hate had blanked out meticulous planning. There were no clues to implicate Clarke. On the other hand, anything of real value left at the scene, would have been purloined by Skillet, he was that kind of cop!

Dead or Alive
— Doc Quaid

He came outside and slowly wiped the sweat from his neck with a large red handkerchief, which he kept in a jacket pocket of his cotton suit.

Saturday had been a long hot Minnesota day, without a trace of breeze which carried through to Sunday morning. Even at that early hour the reflection of sunlight from the white painted woodwork of the granary hurt his eyes. The sickly smell of a rotting corpse in this heat turned his stomach. He never got used to premature death.

Only a few minutes earlier, Doc Quaid drew back a worn piece of calico to uncover a body that lay half hidden amongst a mountain of stored grain. At first it was difficult to assess the situation. Only an arm and leg protruded. As he pulled the head forward, a trickle of grain spilled downwards into the cleavage of a pink blouse. The victim was a woman.

About an hour earlier, he had received a call from Skillet, the Deputy Marshall. All seemed routine, until he reached the farm. Doc had been Coroner in that small town called Excelsior, on the edge of Lake Minnetonka, for as long as anyone could remember, and had acquired a feel for felony. Instinct told him this was something different.

Skillet waited outside. As Doc approached he pushed back a wide-brimmed hat from his forehead, folded his arms, and leant against the wing of his black 1955 Ford Mainline Tudor police car.

'Is it her, can you confirm it Doc?'

'Confirm what?' Came the reply.

'Is the stiff that famous actress? The Hollywood Star from the Big White House. It's her Cream Packard over there, how long has she been dead?'

Doc was used to this approach and deliberately slowed his response. Snap judgements were like tablets of stone to Skillet.

'Difficult to say in this heat. A detailed examination is required.' Slowly, he took out a worn tin box,

THE CREAM PACKARD

extracted a pinch of tobacco, stuffed it into an old hickory pipe, jabbed the other end into the corner of his mouth, and lit it. He blew the smoke Skillets way. The Deputy ignored the insult.

'Come on Doc. The Captain will be here soon; for the love of God, give me some answers!'

'Her name is Elaine Mason,' said a voice that came from someone in his early thirties. He wore a short-sleeved shirt, loosened at the collar, with grubby faded green tie, and carried a jacket over one arm.

'The name is Johnson, Matt Johnson, press, *Minnesota Star.*'

'And your interest?' Doc enquired.

'Cover story, public interest ; local girl does good, or bad some would say.'

'How come you got here so damn quick?'

'Just passing through, saw the commotion, and stopped by. Sunday is a dead day for news, if you don't mind the quip.'

Doc looked dubious. No surprise there...Skillet phoned Johnson earlier with news of the event and got a kickback for the effort.

'Was she suffocated Doc, with all that grain on top of her? What a way to make an exit, just like an actress.'

Doc glanced at the reporter with contempt.

'Is that all this means to you? A Goddamn newspaper headline. We are talking about a life here!'

A tall, gangly, thin man, with a worn face and worked hands came alongside them.

'Gee Doc, honest, I didn't know she was there, in the granary, swear it. I've told those kids a thousand times not to mess with the hopper. The trap must have opened and brought the grain down. I knew nothing until Skillet arrived and told me he was looking for a body. The wife won't like it one bit.'

Skillet fumed.

'Don't anybody in this County call me by my proper name? Even Marshall would do once in a while!'

'Take it slow, Jacob,' said Doc. 'Not your fault. She was dead long before the grain covered her. Hear anything last night?'

'Our dog barked late. An almighty din, woke me up, looked out but saw nothin.' Jacob pointed across the field.

'Is that Mason's Packard over there, beside that line of trees? Gee, those white wall tyres sure are handsome…maybe get some for the tractor!'

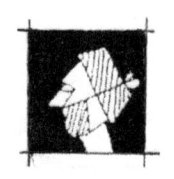

Autopsy
– Clarence Larson

Doc was annoyed when they placed the body on the slab Monday morning. Given another day he would have been on his way to Canada for the annual fishing trip with Herb Macinley, owner of the local hotel.

Clarence Larson, Hennepin's Medical Examiner, stood over the victim.

Wearing a dark green rubber apron and surgical mask, he started to dissect and analyse the evidence. From the outset, he noticed her hair was damp and lay flat across her forehead.

'No doubt about it, she died from drowning, probably lake water. No obvious marks, save for a bruise to the right temple. Further tests will have to be carried out, you understand.'

'In case she was poisoned?' asked Doc.

'So we are absolutely sure there was no foul play. For now, you can be sure she drowned.'

'Could she have been hit?'

'More of a glancing blow than use by a heavy instrument. She may have collided with a wooden object in the water. There are fragments of splinter in her hair. Three fingernails on her right hand are broken.'

'Could she have been pushed into the water?'

'Good question, but not for me to say. Did you know her?'

'Yes I knew her. Watched her grow up, ride her ponies and sail on the lake. She enjoyed life. Her name was Caroline Mason. I will need your report soon, Clarence. This looks a tricky one.'

As he moved towards the door Clarence Larson removed his mask and apron.

'Could be,' he replied. 'One more thing ; she was pregnant, about five months gone, I would say!'

JULIE

'Caroline was so kind, she let me work all the horses with her. I expected her at the stable this morning. She never missed Sunday mornings, that is when we cleaned the tack.'

The Deputy Marshall was determined to get some answers.

'Tell me about Saturday.'

'We were at the State Fair, preparing for the main evening event.'

'Anything unusual that day?'

'It was mostly routine, but she gave me her favourite Mexican Silver Saddle. She loved that saddle, said it brought her luck. Had me polish it a few times, but I didn't mind the work, if it pleased her. Strangely, she felt unwell, so I rode Waxwing in the contest that night. We won, you know, the Blue Riband. Do you think I should have accepted her gift, when it meant so much to her? Did I do the right thing?'

'Sure you did, she wanted you to have it. What a nice gesture. Treasure it!'

'One more thing, Marshall, before we left for the fair, Caroline repeated the feeding and exercise schedules for the horses. I thought that unusual because I know them by heart. When I arrived here this morning all of the photos had been removed from the walls, which upset me. Some showed us both holding trophies.'

Mae appeared and overheard the interrogation.

'Julie is my granddaughter, Marshall. She attends high school and helps out at weekends and holidays. Go easy on her, she's young. This comes as a shock to all of us.'

'No harm intended, only a couple more. What time did she leave the Stadium. Were there any boyfriends?'

'I came out of the ring about ten and she was gone. I used to tease her about Nick, but I don't think they were going steady. Never saw them making out or anything. Heard her on the phone to someone called Britt, they had an argument for some reason or other.'

Skillet ended the enquiry, thanked them both, and left through the courtyard.

THE ALIBI

After speaking to Julie, Skillet walked from the stables to the swimming pool. Warren Clarke climbed out of the water and put on a bathrobe. 'My deep condolences to your family, but you understand there are questions which need answers.'

'Caroline took her own life, Marshall, we both know that, she suffered from depression.'

It was Skillet's turn.

'That part is under investigation, sir. The Coroner will decide the outcome. Can you tell me your whereabouts Saturday evening?'

Clarke was taken by surprise. As parent to the victim he had not expected any tough questions, so had to think fast. Any delay in response would do.

'Would you mind if I got changed first? In the

lounge is a drinks cabinet, help yourself.'

Those precious moments allowed him time to stitch together an alibi. He wanted no connection to this sudden death. Bad for reputation, worse for any potential political career.

* * *

In truth, he had received a frantic phonecall from Caroline around seven thirty Saturday evening. Their relationship was a mess. Money meant little to her, so she couldn't be bought off like all the others. He knew he had to end it, and soon, so used guile and ingenuity when they met at the stables. It was their last encounter.

Clarke broke the news gently, as best he could, but Caroline was having none of it. She was in one of her mood swings. Clarke knew her condition and had taken advantage, with or without her consent. A shoulder to cry on had quickly developed into sexual gratification. In her state of mind he had all but destroyed her.

The meeting became a screaming match, and Caroline was making the most noise. She threatened to go to the police.

'There must be some law that prevents a step father taking advantage of his bloody stepdaughter!' she exclaimed.

For once the cool calculating Clarke could not handle this situation. The affair had turned septic. He left the stables and headed for the nearest Jack Daniels.

*　*　*

Clarke returned, casually dressed and confident.

'All Saturday I was with a friend, Marshall, and that includes Saturday night, if you know what I mean'…

'May I ask her name, sir?'

'Lisell, but you understand this is a delicate matter.'

'Then let me ask you another ; did Caroline know anyone called Britt or do you know anyone by that name?'

Clarke wasn't sure where this was leading, but disguised any giveaway.

'How clever of you Marshall, her full name is Britt Lisell.'

The next question stunned him.

'Could she have been Caroline's psychiatrist?'

Until then he had played Skillet for a fool. It was a rash assumption.

'Not sure, she never disclosed any of this to me. Thought her depression had played out, not left to linger.'

Skillet took further details and left. A stunned Warren Clarke grabbed the nearest phone to call Lisell.

'I need an alibi. Skillett is on his way over. Tell him I was with you all Saturday. It's about Caroline, she was found dead this morning!'

* * *

Britt Lisell took advantage of Clarke's phonecall. As predicted, Skillet arrived within the hour. She confirmed her tryst with Clarke, but declined to divulge Caroline's medical history. *Thank God,* she thought, *Skillett never asked for more details.* In fact she had no choice. The truth was more complicated but for now she would cover for an old friend. A strange twist meant his alibi became her alibi, as long as they both stuck to the same lie.

Events had overtaken her plan to implicate her lover in the death of his stepdaughter. They both had alibis, but he had the edge. Should she try and implicate him, he would turn her in on a kidnap and extortion charge. The police would also indict her for murder. For now, her plot had failed.

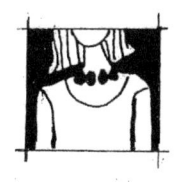

Man Bites Dog

Johnson and Hogarth drove out to the Big White House on Monday to capitalise on the scandal. He looked pleased.

'I feel confident we will get an exclusive from Marcia Clarke, maybe even Caroline, if our luck holds. I phoned through Sunday morning and gave the office the headline.' Hogarth had already seen the *Star* front page, which read 'Elaine Mason Murdered'. She withheld her congratulations because Johnson had not invited her along to the crime scene Sunday morning. He made the excuse that it was all too gruesome, and that the Police would not permit photos. *Fat lie,* she thought!

Two police cars were parked in the drive as they arrived. A maid answered the door, showed them into

THE CREAM PACKARD

the living room, and reappeared with coffee soon after. Johnson moved outside onto the patio for a cigarette. The maid returned.

'There is a call from your office Miss Hogarth. Will you take it here?' Hogarth picked up the phone.

'Mac here, remember me? Get that baboon on the phone, I want to speak to him. He's in deep this time!'

'Sorry, Mac, he's just stepped out. Can I help?'

'Tell him he's toast! If the Clarkes sue, the *Star* is finished.'

'So what is the problem?'

'That idiot has got the wrong body again!...... It's Caroline who is dead. Elaine is alive and probably sipping champagne as we speak. It's bedlam here. The Mayor rang me. He thinks Johnson did this on purpose. Tell him to call me!'

The phone went dead. Hogarth drank the remains of her coffee and smothered a broad grin. She never mentioned the phonecall, but held out long enough to get a reaction and payback.

Johnson came inside and closed both French windows. He sat down, nibbled a biscuit, but ignored the coffee. The sound of voices in the hallway tailed off as the police left and the front door closed. Elaine

Mason entered the room wearing her familiar amber bead necklace. Johnson's biscuit fell from an open mouth.

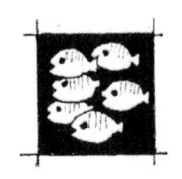

Sunfish

Doc Quaid met Herb Macinley Monday evening for a spot of fishing. Herb owned the local Hotel, and coming up to retirement was looking to sell the business. Trade had been slow this season. Doc thought Sunfish a poor substitute. The fat, juicy Canadian salmon would have to wait a while longer on account of the sudden death and enquiry.

'This scandal does nothing for the hotel trade, it's caused quite a stir in these parts,' said Macinley.

Doc moved into deeper water and recast his line.

'It sure sells newspapers, the press were onto it like flies on fresh dung. Maybe you are in the wrong trade. Mind you, they got it all wrong again, always jumping to the wrong conclusion.'

Herb reeled in his line and examined what was left of his bait.

'Never met the actress, but she was at the hotel a week ago. There was an almighty argument and damage to the room which my cleaner discovered next morning.'

'Can't say I've met her either,' replied Doc.

Herb let his line drift.

'But you saw her, didn't you? Lying in the granary?'

Doc looked hurt and cut him short.

'Don't believe all you read. Everyone assumed it was Elaine Mason on account of the Packard nearby. Even fooled me for a while. The victim was her sister Caroline.'

'Was she murdered?'

'You are an old friend Herb, so let me tell you I'm conducting an enquiry, and the autopsy is the cornerstone of any investigation. It's methodical, lengthy and tedious. Most errors are often buried or cremated. It's ongoing, which brings me back to your hotel. On the night of the storm, did anyone spot the driver of the cream Packard. Did anyone actually see Elaine Mason at your hotel?'

'Well, since you put it that way, I guess not. But everyone saw the cream Packard!'

FBI
– Novak and Petersen

Wednesday morning, Nick reversed the Packard from the barn, only to check the fuel levels. Josh did all the regular washing and knew all about the creams and polishes, so he didn't want any errors or tread on the old boy's toes.

Suddenly, a black 1951 Studebaker four door land cruiser sedan came alongside. Two men in dark overcoats got out and approached Nick. One held out a badge.

'Novak, FBI, that's my partner, Petersen. Can you step into the car, Mr. Carter? We want a word with you.'

'Am I under arrest?'

'Not yet, but it's in your own interest.'

'I need a lawyer, get me a lawyer!'

Novak stared coldly ahead.

'Mr.Carter, I think you have been watching too many movies of the wrong kind. Let's talk first.'

There was a grain of truth in what this guy said, thought Nick, who had seen every conceivable gangster flick featuring Cagney and Bogart, including Johnny Huston's *Maltese Falcon*. Nick took the short route and got into the car.

'Listen up,' Novak began, 'we want your cooperation.'

'I'm here on vacation, what is this? A murder wrap?' Novak smiled.

'Elaine Mason is up to her neck in an illegal sapphire racket. The gems are coming in tax free through Chicago. At first we weren't sure, but last week's auction clinched it. We know you were there. As an accomplice, you could face a ten stretch in Quentin. It's a promise you won't like the food or the company. We hear they don't throw away the keys because there are none. They incarcerate inmates with an acetylene torch. No way out!'

'That bad?… Go on I'm all ears.'

'It was a syndicate operation. Highest bidder got the goods.'

'Sounds unlikely, why not offer them all a private deal?'

'They tried that a while back. It ended in a messy shoot out when one dealer got greedy.'

'So it was a crooked auction, within an auction, and the guy with the gavel was in on it?'

'You are doing swell kid, maybe those movies are doing some good after all.'

'How was I to know? I only drove her car. Do I have a choice in this?'

'Frankly, kid, you don't!'

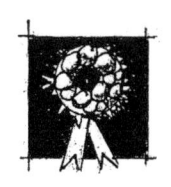

Funeral

Friday morning, the first wild geese began to gather on the lake to signal the end of summer. Early sunshine gave way to low, overhead clouds, and a cool breeze across an otherwise deserted lake. A hearse followed by two black funeral cars slowly moved through the cemetery. This was Caroline's funeral, and they buried her that morning.

An earlier inquest decided the verdict was "suicide" and she was returned to her family for burial.

Nick Carter was impressed by the dignity of the occasion. He held little Phyl close, and attached his own tribute to an enormous family wreath, adding a single white rose, sealed with a kiss.

Bright as sunshine in early June
A life cut short all too soon.
No more sorrow
No more fears
Sadly, no more laughter
Only our tears.
One brave lady
That part is true
Farewell lovely Caroline
Cherished memories of you.

Following the service, Julie approached Britt Lisell and pressed a plain brown envelope into her hand.

'Caroline left this for you, only discovered it this morning at the stables. Almost gave it to the police, but Grandpa said it was addressed to you, so you should get it.'

Lisell opened the envelope. The text was almost incoherent, but four words were crystal clear ; 'Warren Clarke seduced me.' She moved to the graveside where she met Hogarth and erected an umbrella as the first rain appeared.

'Let's talk in the car. I have something you want… but at a price.'

Body Snatchers
– Nick Carter

I'm not exactly sure how it came about on Friday night, but Matt Johnson's power of persuasion had me exchanging one body for another at Oakwood Care Home. A distant uncle once told me that the burial business was lucrative, but Johnson's offer of a meagre five dollars made tonights work less than profitable.

'Who's the 'stiff'?' I enquired, as we moved the casket through the tradesman entrance. I always thought it was *one way* traffic from these places. This exchange must be a first!'

Johnson announced our arrival to a nervous Britt Lisell who was waiting for us.

'Who the hell is he?'…I could feel the warmth in her voice.

'Don't worry ; that's Nick, my driver. He will be back in England next week, well away from all of this.' That part was true. After driving the smooth Packard, taking corners with a hearse and coffin was like an episode from Keystone Cops!

'Look sharp, get it inside quickly' came the next order. The weight almost buckled me. I realised then that everything in America was double the size of everywhere else, and this casket was no exception!

'Quit moaning, it will be lighter on the return, for sure,' said Johnson.

We lifted the heavy oak casket onto the table but couldn't empty it.

'Must be rigor and mortis,' I ventured, 'or Laurel and Hardy. Tip it on it's side and let gravity do the rest.' It worked, and Lisell gave us the next instruction.

'She's in the laundry room, be careful with her.'

Mary looked drowsy as we bundled her into the empty casket, and pushed her into the rear of the hearse.

'What about the Death Certificate?' Johnson asked.

'Idiot! You are not burying her, make sure she keeps breathing.'

We left Lisell and "as arranged," dropped off Mary

at her "daughter's." She slept through all the excitement. Joanne crept back into bed after attending to her mother.

'What was all the commotion?' a sleepy Colby enquired.

'The undertaker just delivered mother, she will be with us a while. Hope this is all right with you dear.'

'Makes a change…on his next delivery, ask him if he does extra milk and eggs!'

Happy Days
– Warren Clarke

Warren awoke Saturday morning, or let us say his eyeballs moved, but not much else. He heard the sound of a door open, but even that noise was too much for an aching head. There was a vague recollection of the night before. Someone had bought him a drink at the Blue Orchid.

'Welcome to Oakwood, we hope you will be happy here.'

'Is that you Britt? Thank God, I thought I had been kidnapped.'

'We don't use that word here, we are more sophisticated.'

'I can't move a muscle. What is this contraption I am in?'

'You have been a naughty boy, it is for your own protection.'

She turned to leave.

'Administer the usual medication nurse, but double the dosage, we may have trouble with this one.'

Confined to that small anonymous room, Warren started shredding sheets in frustration. Without bed linen, he froze with the onset of a Minnesota winter. He joined the art class, where, from necessity, (you've guessed it) he was "encouraged" to sew the sheets together again.

Warren made several attempts to escape, even got as far as the main gate. These events always happened on Saturdays when the Drug store offered a special double hamburger and relish. Lisell organised a weekly order from the Cook, delivered with, as she described it, "a special treat of tomato ketchup", providing he had been really nice to the nurses. This curtailed further attempts to abscond.

After a while he joined the art class, but made little progress. Always the same boring sketches…a big white house with the 'stars and stripes' alongside.

'That was my house', he confided to one nurse. ' I used to live there.'

THE CREAM PACKARD

'Yes I know, honey, we all live in white houses in Hennepin County,' came the frosty reply.

Warren was encouraged to grow his hair and soon had a long white beard. In truth it was a labour saving device for the staff. His physical frame became weak, through lack of exercise, so he was wheeled into the common room daily to join the others. There were no visitors. The only clue to his whereabouts came in the obituary column of the *Star*. For once Johnson got it right…well almost!

A year after his admission, Britt Lisell resigned her position and left Oakwood. At a leaving party, the staff presented her with a beautiful bouquet of red gladioli and a set of skis for her return to Sweden. Before her departure, she asked all the staff to take special care of her "dear uncle Warren" and "to make sure he did not wander off". Warren got only one Xmas card. The envelope had a Stockholm postmark and read "always in my thoughts Caroline".

First Love
– Nick Carter

After my brush with the FBI, I was beginning to think this vacation was about to fracture. I was fast becoming a 'sardine' in a sandwich. The FBI option was like toothache. I couldn't stand the pain but hated the thought of an extraction.

Elaine left me sore by flying off like that, but who cares? She gave me a ticket for the State Fair. Maybe I should have headed for the nearest airport with my scalp intact. Hiawatha used to hang out in these parts not long ago.

They say you always remember your first love. Well, that summer it was no contest, given a choice between Betty Higgins, who used to lend me her only Joe Stafford vinyl, and a famous film star. Besides,

Betty's pig-tails weren't long enough and I never liked the colour of her ribbons.

* * *

It was Josh who brought me back to reality, late Thursday morning.

'Elaine wants to see you down at the jetty, needs a hand.'

Her *Cessna* was tied up and she was refuelling.

'Are you migrating with the geese?' I enquired.

'Soon, Nick. A part beckons in a new movie called *Some like it hot.*'

'Is that a lead?'

'Hell no', she replied laughing, 'Monroe has that slot, but it pays the rent.'

'They say Curtis and Jack Lemmon are in it.'

'Now that should be fun. Good for you, Nick. Pleased to hear you are taking an interest, something to take back on your return. Shooting starts in Hollywood then we move down to Coronado Beach, Santiago. With Caroline gone, there won't be a lot for me around here. Soon mother will close the house for winter, then she will fly south to our place in Fort Lauderdale. You could visit her there sometime.'

'Level with me Elaine. The FBI caught up with me this morning. I know all about the sapphires…are you in some kind of mess?'

'Sorry, Nick, I never wanted you dragged into this. Murky's mob are closing in on me, I have to leave.'

'So how does the FBI figure in all this, those two guys who paid a visit look like they mean 'business'.'

'What did they look like?'

'One tall, one short,' was the best I could offer.

'Novak and Petersen, by any chance?'

'The same, how did you guess?'

'No surprise. They're with Murky, not the FBI. Novak used to work for Chicago Police until they caught him operating a scam from Detroit. He's on the 'wanted' list. Petersen is the one to watch. Used to work for the Merelli Mob.'

'How come you know so much?'

'We get all the slime through the culverts of Los Angeles. East dumps on west. If you still like me Nick, listen carefully. Here is what I want you to do!'

The Setup

As arranged on Mason's advice, Nick phoned Novak on Friday night.

'I have the information you want. All you have to do is be there and make an arrest. She will be at a house called Motola to collect her paintings, plus the Caravaggio. The house is on the lake, about half an hours drive. It is empty. One more thing. Her driver is elderly and no problem. It will be dark, but her cream Packard is easy to follow.'

Late Saturday, Nick caught Josh at the barn just before he closed up. It had been a long day. One of the horses had fallen into a ditch and the vet called. It took almost all afternoon to rescue the animal.

'Elaine wants you to deliver this package. It's not heavy.'

'Can it wait till morning Nick? It's getting late.'

'Sorry Josh, it's important, must be tonight. She says to take the Packard and deliver it to Motola. Be sure to take Mae with you, she will enjoy the drive. It will get cold later, so she has sent a silk scarf for her to wear, a gift for the occasion.'

Josh was surprised at the late hour of the request, but ecstatic at the prospect of his first drive. He left the barn doors ajar and rushed off to tell Mae, and pass on the gift.

'Are you coming along, Nick?' he called back.

'No, she's all yours tonight. Enjoy your trip and tell me all about it tomorrow. One more thing, nearly forgot, when you get to the house, open the front door and leave the package on the hall table.' Nick phoned Hogarth.

'I've been trying to reach Matt since five o'clock. Where is he?'

'Probably at the Drug Store talking to Shelli. They are getting close, those two.'

'Forget his love life. If you want a scoop, get your boyfriend to Motola tonight. Be sure to bring your camera. Tell him he can buy me a soda later!'

The Fix

The Cream Packard left by the main gate. By now it was nightfall, and colder. Josh kept the hood up and switched on the large headlights which picked out the road ahead, edged by high grass and trees.

Further along, a black car slowly moved in the same direction, at a discrete distance. There were four passengers inside the 1949 Buick Super Serie 50 limousine.

Murky sat in a rear seat with Santiago for company. He had travelled from Chicago to fix this deal, and "eliminate this broad." Murky was a sore loser. In his words, "a cold, dark night was perfect to rub out a Hollywood queen." It had been a tedious wait. Mason had made no contact, he would give her a surprise!

'Are you sure it's her in the Packard?' he asked Petersen his driver.

'Sure boss, she's wearing a headscarf, but is the only one who gets to ride in her precious Packard.'

'If that's her mother in there, you had better look for a new set of balls. Your track record hasn't had any home runs of late!'

The Packard moved along at a steady pace. Josh was enjoying his first solo ride.

'Take it easy,' broke in Mae, 'there is a big engine under this bonnet.'

He smiled. The old girl was right, but he knew more about the second love of his life than anyone else, and was in no hurry to rush his first drive.

Mae navigated.

'Take the fork at the next junction. The house should be down there. We had a church picnic a while back, seem to remember a building at the end of the lake. It was blue. Yes, pale blue.'

'What is the good of telling me the colour at this time of night?' he replied. 'Give me the name again.' Further into the trees, along a disused track, the headlights picked out a weathered wooden sign which read "Motola".

'Strange name, are you sure this is it?'

'Keep your eyes ahead, we are almost there.'

The winding track suddenly opened onto a flat gravel forecourt in front of a large painted clapboard structure, surrounded on three sides by a neglected lawn. Josh stopped the car, cut the engine, and got out.

'Want to stretch your legs? This place looks deserted.'

'Are you mad? On this cold night, in the middle of nowhere? Hurry up and drop that package,' she retorted. He removed it from the car, walked to the front door, and rang the bell. There was no answer.

'Open the door, you idiot!' Mae shouted.

He did as instructed and left the package on a table in the hallway. That bit he remembered, but forgot to close the door. Mae spotted headlights approaching along the track.

'Strange that, and they are heading our way, must have followed us. Don't reverse, it's way too narrow to get through. We must have come in the tradesman's entrance. Take a left and follow the drive from the house to the main gate.'

'Shouldn't we wait? It may be the owner.'

'He won't be using this entrance. At this time of

night, it must be someone else. It's way past bedtime, let's go home,' she replied.

As they left, the Buick stopped further back.

'Novak, get out and check this place,' barked Murphy.

'Why me? Let Petersen do it.'

'He's our driver, you idiot! Get a move on. I want this wrapped up before Thanksgiving!'

Novak approached the house. An upstairs light illuminated the hallway and the open front door. He heard a voice, but quickly retraced his steps to the waiting car.

'There is a light on upstairs,' he announced. 'I heard a voice say "welcome, come inside".'

'How come she was expecting us?' asked Peterson.

'The kid must have told her, that's love for you,' added Novak.

Murky discarded his half-smoked Cabras and left the car. Novak joined him as they entered the house. All was quiet as Novak climbed the stairs towards a shaft of light from one of the bedrooms.

'Take a look inside, use your gun if you have to,' screamed Murky.

Novak obeyed orders, approached the bedroom, kicked open the door, and rushed inside. The light went out, there was a scuffle, the gun was knocked out of his hand, and he was entrapped by a pair of handcuffs. Meanwhile, Murky, half way up the stairs, heard the commotion, turned around and ran back to the hallway. Outside the front door, he was confronted by a dark figure holding a gun.

'If that's you, Petersen, get inside and help Novak, she ain't dead yet.'

'No, but you are fat boy!'

The figure moved forward, silhouetted against the lake.

'Same old Murky…drop Petersen in it while you cross the State Line.'

Murky froze.

'What the hell? Is that you Carla? It's not like that, you have it wrong. Go back to the car and we'll get out of here. Mason can wait.'

'Too late for the sweet talk, lover. You have smoked your last Cuban. Goodbye Murky!'

In the darkness, he had not seen the Smith and Wesson 38mm revolver by her side, which she leveled with his chest. Slowly, she squeezed the trigger and fired twice. Each time she hit the target Murky recoiled. The impact oozed blood through his clutching fingers.

His face drained of all colour, as he sank to his knees. She finished him off with a third and final shot to the forehead. Santiago threw the gun into the lake and returned to the car. It was a cold calculated execution.

She calmly closed the car door, then briefly kissed Petersen.

'It's 'payback'. Let's get out of here, hit it!'

Back on the highway Petersen broke the silence.

'No regrets, sugar?'

'Not a grain. Nothing will pay for what he did to my sister, but that's as close as it gets!'

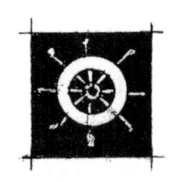

Sweet Revenge
– Carla Santiago

My hate was so intense I could taste it. The moment came, the timing was perfect, it had to be. Any mistake on my part would send me tits up in the Chesapeake, alongside poor Joe. I took my chance but it was a fine balance. Murky had learned a lot from the Merelli Mob. He survived because he trusted no one. My weakness was that I thought I could second guess his every move. When you get close to a mobster, like I did, you quickly learn there is no pattern to the play. The spots on the dice keep changing.

Murky stayed in Chicago while I went to live in Florida. In that short interval, unbeknown to me he set up a narcotics courier racket, which he later transferred to the south coast. I only discovered this by chance when a local cop paid a visit at our villa to demand a percentage of the 'take'. Murky almost blew a gasket, not because of the 'kickback', but because the guy had the audacity to knock on our front door!

For a while, the onshore courier setup took over from fast boats delivering narcotics from Cuba. At least, until he acquired faster craft to outrun the Coastguard. It was never an even match, and a continual challenge. The couriers were Cuban, mostly young women, desperate for drugs, cash, or both. By way of a cover up he even donated a new operating theatre to a local hospital ship. His profile dipped after a patient died through lack of oxygen. The cylinders had been filled with imported heroin. Murky paid his way out of that one dearly.

There was worse to come for me. Our boat was moored at Fort Lauderdale, and sometimes we slept on board, where it was cooler. One night there was an incident that woke us. Two men carried a body on board. An argument started. Murky tried to throw the 'stiff' overboard. From what I heard, the victim had swallowed drugs to bypass customs but had died a horrific, painful death.

They moved into the wheelhouse and left the

body under a sheet of canvas. I realised the situation was hopeless, but could not sleep, got dressed, and climbed the stairs onto the deck. Even in that light, as I removed the cover, I could see it was the body of a young woman. Her hair was dark, like mine, and matted with perspiration. Her face had taken on a paleness, the colour drained from her cheeks. She looked a lot like me. The girl was Zamira, my sister!

Front Page

To close it off, Skillet got an anonymous tip-off and lay in wait for the Murky Mob at Motola. He was pleased to apprehend Novak, whose gun was unlicensed and a separate violation. He faced ten years out of harms way.

Johnson spent too long at the Drugstore with Shelley and missed the shooting but arrived early enough to capture a useful interview with Skillet, following another donation to the widows and orphans fund. Hogarth got realistic shots of a very dead Murky and his accomplice. Good press coverage in the *Star* was a first for Skillet. The front page even managed a photo, but as he told his barber "It wasn't a good likeness"… more of his wide-brimmed hat than any noticeable features.

THE CREAM PACKARD

At Police HQ, Skillet briefed the Chief on the previous evenings entertainment. Skillet said there had been mention of illicit gem smuggling, but he had only found one package, which he placed on the Captains desk.

'So you reckon this is valuable, Marshall?' he enquired. 'We had better open it.'

Skillet obliged by removing a covering of thick brown paper, tied securely with a cord, to reveal a white feathered sulphur-crested Cockatoo in a cage.

'Welcome, come inside, I've been expecting you,' the bird mimicked!!

Au Revoir

Sunday morning, Matt Johnson and Barbara Hogarth packed their bags, settled the bill, and left the boarding house in Excelsior.

'You can give me a lift to the bus stop after you buy me coffee,' she said.

They entered the Drugstore where a distant sound of Gale Storm's 'Why do Fools Fall in Love' played from the illuminated juke box. They sat down either side of their favourite table. Two coffees arrived. He took up the conversation.

'I will be here another couple of days, they need me at the Marshall's office, just routine.'

'Mac will hear all about it, but you'll need a better excuse.'

'Well, … between friends, I want to do a spot of

fishing, and I like the lake people around these parts.'

'You did well to rescue Mary from that care home. I'm almost proud of you.'

'Nick helped me.'

'Sure, but you set it up. Have you thought of the burial business as a permanent career?'

'You may have noticed, young lady, over the past fortnight, I'm already close to being a corpse, and die with every headline!' She laughed.

'Mac seems happy enough with the Elaine Mason spread.'

He lifted a spoon to stir his coffee.

'Sure, … it took us long enough, but it was Caroline's suicide and Murky's murder that took the front pages. You were right all along ; Mason remains an enigma. In this game truth and fiction fuse into the same thing, providing they sell newspapers.'

'I'm not convinced she was at the hotel, or Motola.'

'We were there, we saw her cream Packard, it had to be her, but come to think, she wasn't at the granary Sunday morning…that's for sure.'

'We never found your historical fence.'

'No, but I gave it some thought. The reality was that Mary Christie tried to write a message on her painting, but was too unwell to make it coherent. Colby and I got it wrong. We thought the scribble looked like a fence. I might construct one. It would make a neat boundary around our new back yard.'

'Is that some kind of proposal, Matt Johnson?'

'Maybe, but don't rush your fences, so to speak, remember I'm not good at headlines.'

'We seem to have left out more than we printed… chased a few butterflies without a net.'

'It would make a good novel,' he replied.

Barbara Hogarth drank the remains of her coffee, thanked Shelley, added a generous tip, and left in the station wagon for the bus terminal.

Farewell Minnesota

Sunday morning was crisp. One or two maples were beginning to change colour from yellow to gold with the early onset of autumn. Elaine Mason and Nick Carter were down at the jetty.

'That's the last of the paintings, Elaine. The barn is empty.'

'Any problems last night?'

'None I heard, it went sweet as a nut, just as you predicted. Novak was arrested and you won't be seeing Murky for a while. Skillet got his photo in the press thanks to Barbara Hogarth. Josh and Mae sure enjoyed their ride in your car. Mae thanks you for the scarf, but was curious about the package. Thought she heard a squawking noise.'

'She did. You gave them the wrong package. They

were meant to deliver one of the pictures and implicate Murky. Collect the parrot from Skillet and return it to Joe Evans who supplies pets for the movie business. He asked me to take care of it over the weekend. Such a sweet bird and a good talker!'

'So where is your bag, Nick. Aren't you coming with me? We could explore the everglades together.'

'Not this trip Elaine. You are running way ahead of me. I'm off home to England soon, but will look out for your movie at our local cinema. Maybe next summer I will return, if aunt Marcia will have me, and I'll keep an eye on the lake. Should the mallards screech, it will be a sure sign your *Cessna* has landed!'

She blew a kiss, secured the seat belt, switched on ignition, and guided her aircraft into the middle of the lake. The takeoff was a success as she left the fields of fading yellow sunflowers behind.

Message
– Nick Carter

That night, I switched on the local radio for the last time, and began to drop a few things into a holdall for my return journey. The sound of Doris Day's popular 'Sentimental Journey' came across loud and clear. There was a message there somewhere!

Next came a promotion for Jane Mansfield's film *The Girl Can't Help It,* with an Eddie Cochran backup. I guess Elaine could not help it either…the way she manipulated others for her own ends. She never knew who her real friends were ; maybe didn't care. *Let's face it,* I kept telling myself, *she was exciting, fascinating, and glamorous and had even invited me to Florida, but like the song, it was time for me to make my own 'sentimental journey' home.*

The packing became a bore, so I undressed and climbed into bed but had forgotten to clean my teeth, so hauled myself out again and moved across to the wash basin. My emotions were mixed, and after a quick scrub got back beneath the sheets to lie there a while.

Strangely, I felt something different about the room, almost a presence. It was a small room so there was not much to disarray. The furniture was the same, but I could have made a better job of tidying away my clothes.

A picture on the wall, hung at an angle, looked different, but not obvious. The bottom line of faded wallpaper below the frame also caught my attention, barely visible as moonlight shone through the window. On a darker night it would have been missed. The original had been replaced.

The mystery could have waited until morning, but I am not that sort of guy. The replaced oil looked drab, uninteresting, and not to my taste, but the ornate gold frame was impressive. As I levelled the frame, an envelope, which had been lodged behind, fell to the floor. It looked like Elaine's handwriting and it was addressed to me!

Memories

I never returned to beautiful Minnesota the next summer, but aunt Marcia kept in touch for a while.

Elaine finished her movie which was a box office success, did a couple more, then married a film director. They have one daughter, but got divorced. Last I heard; she appeared in an episode of the Perry Mason show.

Matt and Barbara got engaged but never married. He moved on to the *St.Paul Gazette* after a final fallout with Mac. Barbara left for Denver where she set up an advertising agency. Last call, she was doing well, but still single.

Julie inherited Waxwing and the other horses to start her own riding academy following graduation. She took good care of little Phyl who sadly died one year after Caroline's funeral.

Josh and Mae retired to Mexico. He contacted Alzheimers not long after.

Doc Quaid retired, and after a long vacation in Norrkoping, wrote a best seller on salmon fishing in Sweden.

Clarence Larson took early retirement after marrying a rich widow and left for Florida. Some say he drowned when his boat capsized on a shark fishing expedition. No body was found for the autopsy. Others say his disappearance was a mystery. He had a nagging wife, and a fear of alimony.

Chris Starren entered into a Real Estate partnership. He operates a lucrative sideline in restored vintage motor boats, his first love.

Herb Macinley sold his hotel and moved to Saskatchewan, where he is a part time Ranger.

Vera Pilcher never remarried. She sold the baseball team and set up a charity for underprivileged children. The President gave her a medal for her work. She celebrated her ninetieth birthday last week.

Skillet quit the force after being overlooked for promotion, remarried, and now lives in Wisconsin where he operates a caravan park.

Colby and Joanne settled into their new home and

he opened a practice in Excelsior. They are expecting their first child.

Shelli left the Drug Store, and now works in the Silver Room at Daytons, Minneapolis.

Jacob still lives on his farm. He got a loan to buy a new hopper and now breeds pigs. His ambitious wife persuaded him to open a spam factory. He bought a new tractor *without* white wall tyres.

Mary Christie turned Motola into an Arts and Crafts centre.

Britt Lisell (Mary Christie got a Christmas card) married a paediatrician and opened a private hospital near Stockholm.

Petersen was apprehended and did a five stretch in South Dakota State Penitentiary for illegal import of whisky from Canada. It was rumoured he quietly disposed of his attorney. On release he married Carla Santiago and moved to Las Vegas.

Frankie Bernstein survived the gem racket, opted for a sun tan, holidayed in Vegas, lingered, and went on to develop hotels and casinos after meeting a guy called Petersen. Frankie's second divorce left him a little short, and took away the one thing close to his heart… membership of the Las Vegas Golf Club.

For a while Harry Levene's luck dipped when he went in for a second operation. Following an unexplained rapid recovery, Harry absconded with a curvaceous nurse, and honeymooned in Hawaii.

Novak never saw Christmas… someone took a dislike to him at Livermore.

Murky's body was returned to Chicago for cremation.

A while later, aunt Marcia sold the Big White House and now resides at Oakwood where she occasionally plays scrabble with Warren Clarke. They don't share a room.

And the cream Packard? Well, I am not sure what became of that fabulous car. Maybe one day I will return to Minnesota, and tell you all about it…